FALLING SILVER

FALLING SILVER

**Book One
of the
Rising Bloodlines Trilogy**

A.M. Ross

Table of Contents

This book was begun on a dare.

Dedicated to my fellow writers, who in the midst of suffering rejection after rejection, encouraged—no, actually dared—one another to write something completely out of our respective comfort zones. Each of us has subsequently been a beta reader for each others' projects, and all have found success in our various endeavors. Therefore, to Nicole Villacres, fantasy writer; Emma Scott (a.k.a. Jennifer Ripley), international-romance star; Karen Fayeth, blogger, journalist, author; and Jocelyn Rish, independent filmmaker, whose names I dreaded to see each year in the finals of the annual New York Midnight Madness 48-hour Flash Fiction competition: thank you.

Special thanks go to Emily Mah, Sarah Burr Nichols, Fred Rothganger, and Sherry King from Critical Mass, with beta readers Gail Hildebrand, Rose Wojnar Dillon, Cin Ulibarri, Pat Bartonek Jones, and Deb Harrison, all of whom made this a much better book.

And …

To my family, who have nurtured my imagination.

MYTH OF THE HUNTERS

"If I ever come to kill you, call my name three times."

Karina dived blindly into the brush, Simon's warning howling through her mind as she raced through the deep Minnesota woods with the thing at her back. She slid down a muddy slope and grabbed a low pine branch to break her fall.

The black beast snapped viciously.

"Simon!"

A horrific crunch shuddered through Karina's exhausted body. She clung to the rain-soaked branch, freshly severed from its tree, the jagged end only inches from her whitened knuckles.

"Simon!" Karina's voice sounded strange and high. Did that count as one of three? She shot one last panicked look at the enraged creature's blue-ringed eyes as she tumbled further, the wolf nearly on top of her before she slipped down and out of its long-armed reach. She shouted his name for the third and final time, just as he'd taught her.

Everything stopped.

At the top of the slope, the werewolf's eyes narrowed, and its shaggy head rose to sniff the air. Karina didn't dare breathe.

Had it worked? The glowing eyes returned to her direction as she skidded to a stop, flat on her back. The thing's ears perked up and it began to move toward her.

In a moment, a low snuffling sound came closer ... closer ... She could hear the awful creature slipping down the hill after her, crushing branches along the way. She turned over, buried her head in the damp moss and linked her fingers at the back of her neck in a rigid grip. And there it was, the hot, horrible breath on her collar. Something dripped onto her fingers, and Karina braced for a swift oncoming metamorphosis at the instant the wetness reached her bloodstream. Her stomach flipped and dropped; her heart pounded. Were there any cuts on her hands from the chase? Had a comb scratched her scalp this morning? But there was only stillness, with the sounds of ragged breathing, the hot exhalations on her neck and hands, and cool pine-scented mist.

The enormous man-beast collapsed next to her, nuzzling her shoulder, taking in her scent, almost comforting her. Karina shuddered at the touch.

The night's events crowded her mind: racing to her car, revving it down the dirt road that led to the woods as she tried to chase wolf-Simon away from the danger he was facing; the massive black creature turning on her and raging against her car's windshield; her desperate flight through the backseat passenger window, with the spiderwebbing of the front glass reflecting shards of the full moon, shielding her for a moment.

For that single, guilt-wracked second, she had wished there

really were such a thing as the Hunters, with their rumored silver bullets.

They now lay quietly side by side, the wolf-thing calm but Karina still paralyzed with fear, until just before daybreak when it heaved itself away instinctively and crawled into the undergrowth.

Presently, Simon's human form found Karina again. She had managed to sit up against a tree, but her head was bent to her knees, and her hands were once again clasped tightly behind her neck.

"Karina," he whispered. Her muscles were stiff from the fear and damp chill; she could hardly move in response. Though she cherished Simon's exhausted voice, she could not force her eyes to open to the cold, watery light of dawn.

"It's all right, Karina, you can look at me. I'm decent," he offered with a half-laugh, stroking her hair for a moment before she pulled away.

"Three times—it worked," she responded hoarsely. Simon nodded.

In a few minutes he tugged Karina to her feet. "Come on, you're soaked. You'll freeze to death."

"I'm fine," she responded, her teeth chattering.

"Sure. Come on. I left my moon bag up in that big tree a little way back. There's some dry clothing in it." Simon, in his shredded sweatpants, put an arm around Karina's shoulders and led her through the woods. By the time they reached the big pine where Simon had tossed his belongings, she was numb. Simon hauled on a sweatshirt, but Karina refused his jacket and even swatted off the large towel he offered.

They half-limped the rest of the long and mucky way to Karina's sprawling river-stone cottage, moving quickly past the murdered car with its slashed tires, its bleeding fluid, and the shattered windshield. Karina knew that as the light grew, Simon's impatience with her was deepening, and that he would demand a detailed explanation about her being out in the woods under the full moon. She shakily offered that the damage to the car was from hitting a rock and a tree, and then running off the road, but Simon's patchy nocturnal memory already knew the truth very well.

Within two hours, Simon and Karina were attempting to make everything in the growing morning feel almost normal. Simon jogged over to his quarters, the small log cabin that served as a guest house. Karina, emotionally spent, headed to her own brightly lit bathroom for half an hour under a steady stream of hot, soapy water to wash the night down the drain.

The sunlight was still weak when they reunited in Karina's kitchen. A second pot of coffee was slowly disappearing into their oversized mugs, and a plate of lavishly buttered toast lay untouched on the kitchen table. Their usual banter was gone, along with their appetites.

Now, as she filled Simon's mug again, Karina took his hand in silent apology.

It was killing Simon that she was the one comforting him, insisting that everything was all right and that she was just fine. His throat constricted with each attempt to address the horrors she had faced last night, and her understanding and acceptance of his condition only deepened his pain.

For a change this morning, Karina had permitted Simon's company in the kitchen to let him grind the coffee beans and set out the plates and mugs on the wooden table. It was now two months since his arrival back in Karina's life; he was finally allowed just a little more access to this dominion, since she'd "Simon-proofed" it by selling off the silverware. Karina had ignored his protests that silver was a problem only after he'd turned shape around the full moon. For her sake, he'd managed to rescue some Russian family heirlooms such as sugar tongs and a pastry serving set that had belonged to her great-grandmother. He'd gone with her to the bank to be sure they were locked away in a safe-deposit box.

Eventually, when the coffeepot was once more brewing happily, Simon took a deep breath to broach the subject he had been avoiding. "So, it did work. The name thing."

"Yes. Third time. You were right." Karina paused the brewer and filled his mug for perhaps his fifth dose of caffeine.

Simon leaned forward, arms on his knees, knotting his fingers until his shoulders strained. "I can't even remember where I heard that. Maybe I read it, I don't know."

"It was the looking into the eyes that was the hard part. Lucky for me you only have to do that once. You wouldn't stop dashing around." Her smile was water-colored. "Calling you by name three times was easy."

They were startled by the roar of two or three SUVs pulling up on the tree-lined dirt road that led from the two-lane highway to Karina's house. Heavy footsteps sounded outside, cracking fallen branches in the front yard, and several men's voices called out briskly to one another. A familiar tone squeak-barked above the rest, its owner tromping up the front porch steps as if he owned the place.

Simon knew exactly who this was, and in the meager sunlight, there was still enough wolf in him that he could have snarled and struck his latent claws through the door.

"Oh, no! Let me," Karina caught him by the shirt as they headed through the living room toward the front door. "I want to look him in those beady eyes, and hear him explain to me exactly what he knows about all this."

Deputy Sheriff Bill Moore was standing on the broad porch, jimmying the screen door and calling out authoritatively to someone behind him. Quietly, Karina unlatched the inner lock, waiting an instant, timing it beautifully. Bill shouldered the main door, fell across the threshold and skidded into the living room on his sizable belly. Karina's wool-stockinged foot appeared under his nose. "Get up," she intoned.

Winded, the deputy made no move.

Taken by a spritish impulse, she knelt on one knee and hissed into his ear, "Get up, or I'll bite you."

Deputy Moore had never moved so fast in his adult life. "We thought," he panted, tongue reaching out for the words, "We thought you were ... that the ..."

Simon's temper remained at its edge. "That the maniac had got her? What the …" he finished with a string of epithets and snatched out at Bill's collar. He turned a wide-eyed stare in Karina's direction, a fine ring of blue still circling his brown irises. The hairs on the back of her neck rose again.

"She's here, she's … fine!" squealed the little deputy as he shot to his feet, fled out the door and headed down the steps with the bowlegged stagger of a toddler needing his diaper changed. A lingering pong in the air confirmed the image.

"You'll do *what* to him?" Simon's tone warmed toward Karina, who returned his amused gaze with a startling coldness.

He took a short step toward the window and squinted out, shading his eyes in the still-gloomy midmorning. "Seems that Big Bill has brought along a couple of spooky-werewolf-tale believers. I'll go and talk to them."

"Sounds like it, doesn't it? Wonder where he dug these ones up," Karina grinned at him for the first time that day. "Look, don't dignify these 'werewolf hunter' characters. They're just self-important touro-thugs who have seen too many horror movies. I mean, most people are convinced it's just a crazy homeless guy rooting through the trash and hunting rabbits," Karina jutted her chin toward the intruders. "They'll probably leave with Big Bill anyway. Hey, maybe I should get an actual pet werewolf to ward off trespassers," she mused. "Now, where could I find a really good one?"

Simon grinned, beginning to feel relieved, until out in the

yard a new shape caught his eye. Long and lean, it carried a modified rifle that shimmered with silver inlay in the morning sun. The figure spoke softly to two companions, each dressed the same way, all of them wearing what looked like pairs of large wolf ears attached to their belts.

Simon edged closer to the window, still leery. The three men circled the fenced yard by the woods, picking up werewolf sign and conferring in a close knot. One pointed toward the broad dirt path leading into the woods, and his silver patch caught the light, stinging Simon's eyes.

These weren't the usual local-yokel types that Bill usually rounded up for his "special missions" to locate Bigfoot or chupacabras for crypto-tourists. He could hear these men arguing with Bill about wanting to talk to "the girl in the house," but the deputy was saying something about her not being dressed, and that she hadn't seen anything, and babbling a string of other nonsensical excuses.

Simon heard Karina's quiet footsteps behind him. Too tired for sleep, she had put up her long black hair in a ponytail, ready to begin work. "Are those who I ... For real? With actual badges and uniforms?" she whispered sharply. Her eyes shadowed as she joined Simon at the window to watch the gray-clad men. "Simon, are you all right?"

He hugged her shoulder, ignoring the question. "You'll bite all of them, I suppose?"

"I'll get every single self-important arrogant one of them, starting with Big Bill. And then I'll scratch your furry little head after that," Karina smiled tightly.

"Not behind the ears, remember."

"Simon, seriously, is that really them?"

They watched the strangers climb into one of the heavy vehicles and drive off, Bill gingerly climbing up into another one with the sheriff's shield on the door. Karina shook her head angrily. "Why can't he just stick with the roving-lunatic story and let it go? It's not as if anybody is getting hurt!"

One last look at the now-empty yard confirmed a brief period of safety before Simon's new, daytime nightmare would begin.

The Hunters were very real, and they had arrived.

MEET ME IN THE MIRROR

"I don't know what I look like," began Simon, who had wandered toward Karina's well-lit art studio early in the afternoon and was now leaning against the door. He watched her step back from her enormous easel to critique her own work. "Hey, didn't I put that shirt in the donations bag for you?"

"Well, yes, but it's a bit ratty for them. Perfect for me," Karina responded, wiping an oversized red-checked flannel sleeve across her paint-splattered brow. "As to your first question, you're gorgeous, you look exhausted, and you need a shave," she added. "But you mean ... I guess I didn't think about not ever seeing yourself in that shape. And I wish you'd talk to me about it more," she shot him a disapproving but affectionate look.

"Well ... I do know—a little bit, anyway—how I look at First Night, but not what I was like last night, at Apex." Simon stepped into the large studio, which was lined with canvasses, rags, and pots containing new and old brushes of all sizes. It smelled of water and paint and Karina. "First Night ... there's still some of your own nature that's left, but ... well, you're different, that's for sure, and you feel … you feel as if you could do anything, as if you were invincible. They call it the Rush, that moment when you start to turn shape." He played with one of the large brushes stacked in a pot by the door. "It brings out the worst in you. I mean, if you scare a raccoon, you think it's hilarious and you start howling. Literally, I mean."

"But you aren't really dangerous then, right?"

"I wish. The guy who got me was on the second-last night of the cycle. And I nearly killed him right there. Dropped my tire iron when he bit me and—wham—instant claws." He shook his head. "Turned on him right away, no Rush, nothing. Just a rage."

A half-smile crossed his face as Karina waved him into her studio. "That was Carl … We've actually been friends ever since then. Poor guy was really upset about it next morning. He was a newbie himself, so he couldn't control his impulses very well. A lot of people don't make it past the first few moons, you know? They're crazy with it. Most times they run afoul of another wolf, and it's over. Depending on their bloodline, some even attack their own reflections in water, and they drown. And you know what silver does. That kind of end is rare, though."

Karina had paused her critiquing and was wearing a re-markably understanding expression as she listened.

"If you make it through," he continued, "then after a while, you sense the differences in the cycle. All four nights except Apex you feel it, and it does take you over, but it's still you.

The animal you, on mega-doses of steroids. And then Apex," he paused, "at Apex you lose yourself completely. You'll attack anything that moves."

"And if I'd cut my hands when you drooled on me? If I'd scratched myself on those branches …"

"Any nicks at all and you would have turned on me in a flash. You could easily have killed me right there." He shifted uneasily. "We even have a saying for it. 'New wolves bite hardest.'"

Noting Karina's widened eyes, Simon went on, "But still, even at Apex, you know enough to avoid people, and houses— that whole thing about this Hunter outfit claiming to Silverize your property, it's baloney. Nobody goes near a house—there's nothing there for a werewolf to want. It's the hunt, the chase, the struggle … That's why I went after your car. It wasn't you I was chasing at first." He found himself reddening as Karina's eyes fixed on his, and then she turned away.

To give her a moment or two to absorb his lecture, Simon began focusing on a completed painting she had set aside for a collector. Frowning, he asked, "You're still signing *Redfeather*?"

She nodded with a helpless shrug. "My New York agent said the work would sell faster with a more Native-sounding name."

"The agent you fired?"

Karina shot him a weary smile. "I don't know which of us I hated more. Her for being right or myself for caving in. And it does protect my privacy, in a weird way. Too late now, anyway."

Simon nodded sympathetically, wondering how to pull the conversation back to what she needed to understand. He watched her quietly contemplate what she was developing on her canvas.

"You need to hear this, Rina."

Karina nodded but remained silent.

"Nothing will bring me to this house to break in on a regular wolf night, unless I think you are in trouble. I'm not crashing through windows to 'get' you. I have your scent, and it's embedded deep, as a friend's scent." Karina stiffened at that, but Simon's gaze was distracted by a movement outside the studio. *Just a rabbit. Nothing to worry about.*

"The problem is," he continued, "at Apex, the one full-moon night, if you are outside I will come after you. Maybe just to be near you, that is possible; but at that time, I lose so much control that it's actually possible that you'd be a target. If you run, then you definitely become prey. And why the hell—" Simon finally lost his composure "—were you outside at full moon last night when you *knew* I was around! What were you thinking, Rina?"

"Because Bill told me last night that the Hunters were coming!" Karina rounded on him. "I didn't believe him at first. I thought he was just being hot-air Big Bill with his big important talk, trying to impress some bored local kids in front of me. But then I thought, this time seems different.

What if they *are* real? I had to scare you off and into the woods. I figured I'd be safe in the car! Who knew you would come tearing after it as if it were some giant firetruck for you to chase like an overgrown manic puppy!"

"When did you leave the car?"

"When you were busy chewing off the tires and trying to eat the windshield wipers. It was my only shot."

"And you thought that was a good idea!" snarled Simon.

Karina was now standing inches from him, furious. "This is not my fault!" She shook her paintbrush at Simon, splashing tiny scarlet puddles everywhere. "Don't even think about blaming me."

"Calm down," Simon instantly regretted the worst two words he could have said. It was another few minutes before Karina would speak, and she spent them picking up her brushes and scrubbing them until they squealed with the pain of it.

"I'm sorry," Simon offered gently.

"Oh," Karina glanced at the calendar, where the full moon cycle was marked; this month, by pure chance, it preceded her own personal one. "Sorry, too," she mumbled. "Well, Simon, really!" Her indignation was followed by a giggle, and she pointed a clean wet brush at the calendar. "Why am I arguing with the only man who 'gets' it? The whole PMS thing. Pre-monster syndrome."

Simon chuckled warmly and deeply, and Karina melted, aching for him. He stepped back a pace, his eyes reminding her, "Don't fall for me, Rina," echoing a long-ago conversation from the year she was just growing into womanhood.

She couldn't sustain his gaze. She gestured toward a mirror that hung on the far wall of the studio, reflecting the full afternoon light. "Come over here and sit down," she said gently, "and I'll show you what you looked like last night."

Simon pulled over a tall stool. Once she'd positioned him, she stood beside him and, glancing back and forth between the glass and his face, began to paint over his reflection. A pale gray outline of his face and features took shape on the mirror. "All right ... here's you at the moment."

Darker paints appeared on the glass, adding dimension, as she peered over his shoulder at eye-level. "And now ..."

Something primeval began to emerge in the reflection. It had a flattened crown and a protruding face, with deep furrows where the human creases already were; then, an elongated, broad snout replaced Simon's nose and mouth, and its leathery lips curled back from lengthened, sharpened teeth. He was soon covered in shaggy, spiky hair, his ears grown large and pointy, standing out like demonic horns.

But the eyes ... they were his eyes, and Karina had positioned him so that he was looking into his own face. These eyes, pale-blue ringed, were hooded by the upper lids with vicious folds of brow skin that covered the top halves of his irises. He looked psychopathic, dull-witted, brutish.

White-faced and looking heartbreakingly like a hurt and bewildered child, Simon turned to Karina. She softly brushed the sandy hair from his eyes with her left hand and pulled him to her shoulder, as he raised an arm to hold her in a half embrace. Picking up a wet rag with her other hand, she blurred and washed away all the evidence in the mirror, wishing she hadn't picked up her cherished brushes at all, and feeling herself something like a monster.

Man Feast, Hold the Cheese

"You're late," stated the sheriff, "and I don't want to hear it. You have a job to do here."

Bill slinked through the peeling green door of the small sheriff's station and slid awkwardly into his place at the dilapidated desk, muttering about having had to change clothes and earning himself an icy stare.

"I *was* on business," he protested, glancing at the irrefutable 2:30 p.m. displayed on the wall clock. "I was assisting Adam Hunter's guys."

"I said you have a job to do *here*. Quit mooning around after the pretty painter lady and that pack of Sasquatch-chasing vigilantes and get yourself some dignity," Sheriff Langston handed Deputy Moore a report form. "Go find out what happened to that smashed-up car in the woods out near the creek."

"I'm telling you, Sir, it was a were—"

"No such thing. Those Hunter idiots are a publicity stunt for the big silver outfits. Hey—why don't you hang some garlic 'round your neck as well, keep the vampires away, too?" Langston laughed to himself, "Damn' idiots. 'Werewolves,'" he mocked. "'Silverize your property!' Get a freaking grip, Deputy."

Crimson and tight-lipped, Bill snatched the form and stormed through the tiny office, past a caged cell containing a toothless old derelict the sheriff was holding for vagrancy, out into the muddy street and straight up against Karina, who recoiled.

"Deputy," she acknowledged.

"Miss Redfeather. I was just coming to find you. About your car ..." Bill spun on his heel and followed her back into the sheriff's office. "Tell him. *Tell him*," he jabbed a finger in Langston's direction, "what happened to your car."

"Deputy," Karina smiled coolly, "I was actually looking forward to *your* report on the matter."

"*As was I!*" Langston chased Bill back toward the door, where he lingered as Karina asked about standing bail for the inmate she identified simply as "Old Jake." She gestured gently to an old vagrant who was curled up in a corner softly singing nursery rhymes to himself.

"You can't save 'em all, honey, er, Miss Redfeather. But, since you know him, if you can put him up and keep him off my street, well then—*Deputy!*"

Bill shot off toward the diner, a classic 1950s-era place down the slushy highway that ran through what there was of Pigeon Creek; the tiny village was little more than an upscale truck stop on the northernmost edge of Minnesota. The luxurious, ostentatious cabins and beautifully appointed little cottages ensconced in the wilderness sheltered a fair number of reclusive creative types and the odd philandering politician. Perfect for Howlers, Adam Hunter had declared upon holding a press conference that morning, and he proceeded to distribute fliers to mostly smirking residents regarding the innovative Silverizing process that could save their homes and families from being ripped to pieces by inhuman intruders. It gave local people something to laugh about for a while, and eventually inspired some bored and curious tourists—the sort who usually passed through town quickly—to stay for an extra night, just to see.

Bill caught sight of the Hunters in the diner window, shouldered a path through the doorway and inserted himself at their red vinyl booth, snapping his fingers and wordlessly stabbing at the table in front of him. The Hunters remained silent, and when Bill's coffee did eventually arrive, he found it somewhat on the cool side.

"Look," Bill burst out, "that artist's cousin, that Simon guy? He's a Howler, I know it." He leaned forward, in *sotto voce*, "And I think he's got her now, too."

"Thanks for the update, Bill." Adam Hunter's pale blue eyes had a chilling, unblinking quality.

"Yeah. Well, whatever I can do to help you guys." Bill raised the mug and a streak of fuchsia on its rim caught his attention. Adam's merriment flashed across his face, and a Hunter whose silver-stitched patch read *Travis Figueroa* observed, "Not your shade, Deputy?"

Bill rose sharply and headed for the door, announcing loudly, and to nobody in particular, "Gotta check out this werewolf attack on a car last night. Hey. You! *No tip!*"

Janine, the apparently guilty party of the two somewhat jaded waitresses who co-owned the diner, ignored him, and both women maintained their gazes upon the lean, dark-haired man at the booth.

The Hunters exchanged glances.

"Well," observed Adam, "guess that's why we came here." The three men stood up, stretched, and were rewarded with a barely audible sigh from Shari, the younger waitress.

"No charge," called Janine, brushing a lock of fading copper highlights from her cheek and waving the Hunters away, blushing like a middle-schooler at their winks and the "Thank you, honey."

"Oh, it's good to be a hero," grinned Figueroa as they paused outside on the diner steps, while their new recruit, a young red-headed man named Reese McConnell, looked slightly embarrassed and made a show of searching for his car keys.

Adam stared after Bill, and quietly whistled a snippet of the deputy's theme from a long-lost TV show. "All the same," he hauled on his jacket, its patch gleaming in the weak sunlight, "if there really were two separate Howler descriptions, we better check out this artist chick and her cousin. Oh, hey," he indicated a young woman exiting the Sheriff's doorway across the road, "that looks like her, from what I hear. Who the—is that mangy old guy her cousin?" The men watched Karina bid goodbye to Sheriff Langston and take Old Jake by the arm.

"Li'l Deputy Bill is worried about *that*?" laughed Figueroa, fondling the wolf's ears at his belt. "Doesn't even have teeth, does it? *Aroooooo*."

The Hunters watched Karina escort the old man toward one of the side roads, and as they moved out of sight, the three gray-clad newcomers ambled in the other direction toward their motel.

Partway up the wooded road, a tall, sandy-haired figure appeared from the brush to greet Karina and her companion. The trio smiled and chatted for a moment. "Rina," whispered Simon, as Old Jake pointed and laughed like a child at a large woodpecker hammering away in a nearby tree. "I saw the Hunters' SUVs behind the motel. They're here for the duration, all right." He turned toward Jake, who was in danger of making himself ill by mimicking the actions of the bird high above him.

"See you tomorrow, Rina," Simon announced so that Old Jake could hear him. "I need to get something into Jake's stomach before sunset. Hey, careful tonight," he half-smiled, "there are were-men around." The three parted ways; Simon and Jake turned back up the road to the diner, where Simon leaped up the steps and entered first.

"It's a man-feast this afternoon," observed dark-eyed Shari appreciatively, "and I saw this one first!" she grinned at Janine, who simply rolled her eyes.

"Jake, over here!" Simon dragged Jake's wide-eyed attention from the colorful gumball dispensers by the cash register.

Ignoring Jake's entrance behind Simon, the waitresses agreed that this new customer, Karina's cousin or something, was not one of those regular pretty boys. A square-jawed, broad-shouldered manly-man type, he had probably come to Pigeon Creek to join the Hunters. He looked the part, that was for sure.

"A real man-feast, yes, it is," Shari repeated, seating her customers and languidly producing a menu.

"Miss," Simon grinned ruefully, "You have no idea."

OLD JAKE

"How did you say you met Karina?" Simon turned from watching rainbows drip from icicles spiking the eaves, and addressed his companion, who was gummily grinning across the diner's splattered table.

"She gib me a sammich." Old Jake was a longtime acquaintance—many decades now—in the oddest club of misfits that Simon had ever known.

About twenty-five percent of the food on the worn wooden spoon Jake carried with him never made it to his mouth, and he had no compunctions against talking with whatever was in there at the time. Though Simon felt a great deal of affection for this weakest member of the pack, he still preferred to concentrate on something else while his friend attempted to make a meal. He turned back to try and find shapes in frost patches along the puddled roadway. "When was this?"

"Oh, well," slobbered Old Jake, "she was just about 'lebben or twelb at the time, she tol' me, so … about semty-fibe year ago, now?"

Simon smiled, raided the paper napkin holder without looking and gently tossed a pile across the table. He examined a "Lost Yorkshire Puppies" sign which was freshly taped to the wall above the table. "More like fourteen years, Jake."

"Huh. You sure? Feels like semty-fibe." Jake belched and Simon held his breath for as long as he could. "I saw her today!" Jake continued, and frowned. "She looked young."

"She told me about that. She thought you might need a hand."

"Me?" Jake pushed the bowl away, finally. "Don't need nuttin'. Found me a chipmunk or two for a snack last night." He grinned emptily. Simon sighed. Chipmunks, Yorkie puppies, they all tasted the same after a while.

"Jake, why don't you let me take you to the dentist?"

"Ain't goin' near no sibber filling, Simon, you tryin' to kill me?" The hurt in Jake's eyes hit Simon in the stomach. He made another attempt to explain that techniques had changed, but Jake wasn't going to hear it. "They put sibber in 'em," insisted Jake, "an' you know what happen' then. Whoosh." Chili splattered everywhere, across the table, onto the ceiling and all over the picture of the missing Yorkies. The thought flitted into Simon's mind that the photo probably looked more accurate now, but he brushed it away.

Shari brought over some damp bar rags and threw them on the table with an "I'm-not-doing-it" look.

"It's not like that now," Simon mopped up what he could as Jake interrupted, "Don't you tell me that. One lick o' sibber and—you know." He sat back, arms crossed and nodded several times at Simon. "You seen it." Simon didn't answer.

"Right. That's cuz you know. 'Member Jimmy? 'Member?"

It was decades ago. Jimmy had forgotten to empty his pockets. He was young, and in characteristic exuberance, ripping his way through the woods and thrilling to his own temporary strength, he'd managed to spill his coins and one of them—just one—had been old enough to contain a trace of silver. It slipped across Jimmy's left foot and immolated him. Just like that. Nothing else, not even the dry summer brush, was as much as smoking. Flash. That was it.

From then on, the pack didn't carry anything in their pockets, and some even sewed theirs shut for a while. That practice continued until the underground rumors surfaced that you could tell a werewolf by his empty pockets. For a while, you couldn't hear yourself think for all the fashionable jingling coins, keys, and who-knew-what, even during non-cycle weeks. After that, the members just made sure to gather and check one another before sunset, before heading into the deep northern woods and succumbing to their relentless wildness. It was a ritual they still observed.

The waitress Shari returned with a slightly raised eyebrow and a trash bag into which Simon tossed the filthy rags. He couldn't fault her distaste but it irked him to leave a tip when he'd essentially bussed a couple of years' ketchup and coffee stains off the booth.

"I thought I saw Jimmy last week. You think …" Jake licked his wooden spoon and put it carefully back into his deep overcoat pocket. "What do you think happened to him, anyway?" And he was off, rambling his own deranged pathways, aching without knowing why, chased by the demons of having lived too long and lost too many people.

"I need to wash my hands. Wait for me."

"Simon says? You forgot to say Simon says!" Old Jake shrieked with laughter, regressing two-hundred-odd years to the small child he had been when his bitewolf had got him. Simon touched his arm gently. "Finish your water. Uh, Simon says finish your water."

Jake settled but kept giggling as he slurped. Simon wished he had kept one of the wet rags for his hands, but Shari saw him and brought a couple over. Her look was softer this time. "I got a granddaddy like that," she tossed her head in Old Jake's direction. "Sweet of you to look after him. He your daddy?"

The diner's bell shook above the door as three rifle-slung men seemed to fill the place; the tallest radiated an aura that enveloped the others and their own self-importance.

Hunters.

"Um, uncle," lied Simon. "I need to get him back to the home before they come looking, too. Hey uh, here's a ten. Sorry about the mess," he called behind him, grabbing Old Jake and hauling him through the trio of armed men. He wondered if they really could tell, and something primal in him wanted to growl just to let them know for sure.

"Where we going, where we going?" danced Old Jake, and Simon suddenly regretted the ten dollars' worth of drawing attention to himself. He pushed Jake firmly into the slick parking lot and steadily guided him into the woods. Dark still came early at this time of year.

"Come on, Jake," he soothed once they were in a good two miles, deep and unreachable. "Simon says let me check your pockets."

Boo

Thirty minutes before sunset, one gray flash and then another ducked into the woods behind Simon's guest quarters.

Not Simon and Jake; Karina knew that already. It was not yet dark; besides, even if it were, Simon had once told her that the wolves of his bloodline were black, and Old Jake's were pale gold. Nevertheless, standing before the warmth from the large fireplace in her living room, Karina jumped as the front porch creaked heavily and she heard a rifle cocking.

"I've got a gun!" she lied through the door.

"Adam Hunter, Ma'am."

"Who? What do you want!"

Peeking through the curtains, she saw a gray shape kneel at the woods' edge and take aim with a rifle at something between her cottage and the guest cabin.

"Werewolves spotted in this area, Ma'am. We're here to help."

"What-wolves? Oh, honestly. There's no such thing. Get—"

"Two of them, Ma'am. No joke," Bill's voice chimed in, self-important and, she thought, Big-Bill-ish. "Miss Redfeather—Karina, we are here to protect you. Two werewolves were seen in this area last night, and we think you know that. Frankly," he trailed off as Karina yanked open the front door in disgust, "we thought you could use a little extra help." He recovered himself but began to edge behind Adam as the Hunter tipped his Texas ten-gallon hat.

"Your cousin around, Ma'am?"

"Why?"

"We want to be sure he can handle the situation, Ma'am."

"He's taking a friend over to the V.A. hospital. You missed him by an hour. He'll be back tomorrow to handle whatever you need help with. Thanks for your concern, and have a *great* day."

Adam leveled his gaze on Karina's unfathomable black eyes; so, she was going to play it cool, was she? "Well, Ma'am," he drawled in the deep, honeyed tones his late-night Silverize infomercials played up, "if there's nobody here to look out for you, we'll just stick around." He descended the few steps and nodded, smiling everywhere but in his eyes, and began to walk across the lawn.

A mischievous thought struck Karina as she caught Bill's muddy glare from behind Adam's shoulder, and she jerked a step forward to stamp on the porch. Adam whirled, Bill yelped, and Karina smiled. "Just a spider," she apologized sweetly, and retreated inside, trying not to laugh.

Two werewolves? That was new. They must have spotted Old Jake after all. Bill really did think she was the second one, which was hilarious, but that also meant they suspected Simon as the first, which was not amusing at all. At least this was the final night of the cycle, but she realized with an ache that having drawn this kind of attention, Simon and Jake would need to be on their ways again in the morning.

It crossed her mind to make enough noise inside the cottage to reinforce the men's suspicions about her "transformation," drawing them away from the woods, but she could not be sure that the Hunters wouldn't fire wildly into the house. Any molten silver bullets that hit her would certainly put her out of commission for a while, human or not. And Bill; who knew what or who Bill might fill with lead.

Instead, Karina busied herself making a large vat of cocoa, and appeared on the broad porch with a tray of mugs just as the sun was setting. Sure enough, as soon as the door opened all three rifles and a handgun trained on her. With an inward eye roll—because of course, werewolves would use the door— she gasped, "Oh, did you see something? Is it coming?" and set down the tray with a shade more trembling than was necessary.

Clearly this young woman was as human as the rest of this little gathering, decided Adam, and he leaped up the steps to settle her down. She was a pretty thing indeed, with her waist-length black hair and those Cherokee cheekbones, or whatever they were, and those deeply liquid eyes now touched by tears of gratitude. He knew the effect he could have on women, particularly when he was silhouetted broad-shouldered against the fading light.

"Please don't leave me," she was now begging, and Adam had to swat the infernal Deputy Moore aside.

"We'll be right here, Ma'am, and thank you. Much obliged," Adam waved his team over and introduced them to Karina as she passed out the cocoa. Moore still wouldn't shut up, until Karina gently stroked Adam's silver Hunter's patch with her finger and listened, wide-eyed, as he explained the Hunter mission. Moore looked on in silent fury. For a flash, Adam wondered if this woman was enjoying the deputy's poorly concealed wrath as much as he himself was, but he fell under her charm again as she brushed a wide lock of her hair behind her ear and shyly requested that the Hunters not leave her all by herself tonight, just in case.

The night dragged but the Hunters stayed true to their protective mission, while their beautiful protégée waited quietly inside the cottage, rocking beside the fire, laughing at how easy it had been to keep these self-proclaimed heroes close to the house. She hoped Simon would be able to keep Jake quiet and far away. The fifth and final night left them with their most human mindset, but even Simon's control was shaky at each end of the cycle and she knew he'd be a wild, unstoppable thing if provoked.

Nearly dawn, and there it was.

A manic shriek of a howl that sounded as though it were just outside the house, and the Hunters' adrenalin-infused shouts returned the call. Karina heard orders from Adam, as the Hunters raced into the woods and left Bill to guard the perimeter, which he chose to define as the porch. Only when there was a slight movement of the front window curtain did the deputy sidle down the steps and into the shadow of a massive tree in the yard.

For the first time since the previous evening, Karina felt a deep terror, and the hairs on the back of her neck stood up. There really did seem to be something out there aside from Bill, and even though it was Fifth Night, and Simon wouldn't come in unless—unless what, again?—she withdrew into the inner hall closet and locked herself in. *Look into his eyes and call his name three times, fast, fast, fast because you won't have much time if he gets into the house.*

Bill peeked around the enormous tree trunk, hardly breathing. A rustling nearby, maybe from the window, prevented him from leaping back up the steps—just to see if Karina needed anything. Feeling rather watery, he struggled for control. These were his only clean pants, and he couldn't be late again.

Almost dawn, he thought, and quickly convinced himself that he'd spent the night in the woods protecting a beautiful, grateful woman from a man-eating werewolf. The Hunters remained spread out deep in the woods as the sky began to turn, and the dew fell gently onto Bill's hat. A bit chilly for dew, he thought, and shook it off.

As the deputy strode toward the porch, the wild and hairy version of Simon grew uncomfortable in the low branches below which Bill had been hiding. He dropped silently to the ground and streaked back into the woods to await the sun.

BLOODLINES AND WEIRDOS

"Have you seen the sun?" Simon's slurred voice began to penetrate Old Jake's addled mind. "Jake. Jake! Look up!"

Old Jake's eyes still held a faint outer ring of blue, one of the last vestiges of the night. Jake growled in response, and Simon wheeled him to face the east. The two stood quietly among the trees, breathing and stretching, letting the sun wash over them and restore them.

"Simon! You all right?" Jake's voice broke the quiet. "God, Simon, why don' you get me some teef?" He began to laugh.

"Because watching you try to gum a giant steak is the best entertainment I have." Simon touched his toes, then arched his back. "If we could get a dentist to work on you for three minutes a month, we might be able to do something for you." He watched the blue rings fade in Jake's eyes and knew the brief lucidity was quickly ebbing with it.

"Simon—I smelled Vertigo last night. Watch your back."

That brought Simon up cold.

"Hey," Old Jake said presently, "Hey, Simon! There you are. You came back for me! Seen the sun?" He put an arm around Simon and grinned. "Are we gonna see Karina? I had teef las' night, big ones!" He prattled on as they set off for Karina's cottage and Simon grunted the occasional non-response.

He'd rather face Adam Hunter and a thousand silver dollars than be scented and tracked by Vertigo, King of the viciously aggressive Firewolf Bloodline. Vertigo was Old Jake's bitewolf, the one who caught and tortured him as a small boy and kept him as a pet, a slave, for more than sixty-three years, until Simon's much older pack members liberated and adopted the child from his tormentor.

Simon caught Jake's arm and held him back. A large dark shape was bent over by Karina's porch, beneath the tree, scenting something.

"It' Gregory!" Jake jumped up and down, clapping his hands, "Look, Simon, look! Gregory! Gregory! Seen the sun?"

A huge dark-skinned man stood up, with a welcoming grin that might indeed have replaced the sun itself. Simon could have collapsed with relief, but ran after Jake and mustered the breath to call Karina's name. Greg caught him by the arm and shook his hand, drawing him in to whisper that the Hunters had been and gone. Simon nodded, and the two men followed Old Jake up the porch steps and into the cottage.

Simon had begun to feel that Karina's kitchen was the happiest place he'd ever known, and today it was particularly so as Gregory, chief-elect of what he himself called the "Gang of Puppies," joined them for breakfast.

Karina had decided not to tell Simon about spending the half-hour around sunrise in the hall closet, but she knew from his eyes that he'd already smelled the stale wetness of wool coats and mothballs on her.

"Did your boyfriend protect you from the big bad Hunters last night?" Simon provoked, and Karina aimed a cheeky tongue in his direction, as the happy little group gathered in the kitchen and got a fast breakfast together.

"Oh, I was sooooo scared," Karina replied. "Hunters. Please." Simon and Greg exchanged dark looks and said nothing.

"I have some good news," Karina declared suddenly. "I was awarded that restaurant mural in Duluth! I'll be gone for about three weeks, maybe a bit longer, but I'll see you before next time."

"Congratulations!" "Well done!" "What's a 'muriel'?"

The details emerged before Karina tucked Jake into a cheerfully cushioned daybed in her studio, and sang him an old Russian lullaby she'd learned from her mother. Soon, Greg called her back to the kitchen.

"Karina," Greg began.

Karina warned him off. "Don't, Greg. Not you, too."

"Stop it, Rina, and listen up," Simon snapped coldly, in a tone Karina rarely heard.

"Listen carefully," Greg began anew, his large arms resting on the table. "Karina, Lord knows you have a good heart. But as chief of our little gang of puppies, I am taking you under our collective protection. When you leave here, I'm dousing this place with pepper spray to kill your scent."

Karina looked at him blankly.

"There's a problem. You've been exposed to only a couple of the bloodlines—mine is Earth, and Simon's is Water. But other than Jake, you've never met a Firewolf." Greg's deep voice was chilling.

Karina shook her head, "How many bloodlines are there for this thing anyway, Greg?"

"One for each of the four elements—Simon, aren't you telling her anything?—Earthwolves tend to be pack leaders, elders. Take me; I've been around more than a hundred and fifty years. Then there are Waterwolves like Simon. They can control their impulses the best, and they don't shy away from bodies of water the way the rest of us tend to do." Gregory paused to be sure she was taking it all in.

"And—what—Airwolves?" she cocked an eyebrow.

"The Chimerae." Here Gregory hesitated, knowing how thin the ice was. "But … nobody has ever actually seen one of the Chimerae. Well, one or two reports say they have, but most people, even most of us, wonder if they even exist."

Karina glanced at Simon and was stunned by the lurking animal revealed in his eyes. "Simon—have you seen the sun?" she asked gently.

"Listen to the chief."

"Karina, the most demented Firewolf of them all is in the area. He's known as Vertigo, and his sole joy is to inflict the curse, or to kidnap people and torture them until the moon turns and he can."

The clock struck ten and they all jumped.

"Is that what happened with Jake, then …" Karina gestured in the direction of her studio. Both men nodded grimly.

"Vertigo was Jake's bitewolf; Jake was four years old. Vertigo slaughtered Jake's family out on the Texas plains, and then he kept the little guy as a toy," Simon explained quietly.

"So that's why …"

"Yep." Gregory leaned back. "He's nuts. Demented. Poor Old Jake gets a couple of lucid moments at sunrise, maybe once or twice a month … then he goes into *that* state.

"We take cycles looking out for him." Gregory continued. "Mostly because Firewolves are the most dangerous. A lot of them can't control themselves, but a whole lot more, like Vertigo—well, they just plain like it that way. They're already human psychos who know about the bloodline through word of mouth." He shook his head with contempt. "They want to make the most of the way they already behave. So they actively try to get bitten and that way, they can really go nuts. Weirdos."

"You've never said anything much about Firewolves before, either of you."

"They've usually stayed away from the north. Too cold for them. Don't laugh," Simon raised a warning finger. "Karina, you tend to feed every vagrant, every lost soul who knocks on that door. You have to stop. I mean right now. Vertigo is not

Old Jake."

"Well, there aren't likely to be any wolves of any kind in Duluth, unless you count that sleazy doorman at the hotel. Oh, stop playing big brothers!" Karina snapped at her adopted family. "I need to pack."

Simon and Gregory helped Karina load up her rental car for the trip to Duluth, filling in details and trying to ensure that she was taking the situation seriously. It didn't help when she interjected, "Wait. You're telling me that a werewolf can be warded off with pepper spray?" and burst out laughing. But eventually they packed her off to her new project and worked out their next move between them.

An hour later, Simon was knocking on the door to Adam Hunter's motel room.

"Hey," he said to Adam's startled look, "I'd like to get my cousin's place Silverized."

The Creek Run—Artist Redfeather Has Property Silverized™

Pigeon Creek—Acclaimed painter and sculptor Karina Redfeather is reportedly having her Pigeon Creek house and surrounding property Silverized™, sources say.

Mr. Adam Hunter, whose family owns both Silverize™ and Vortex Oil companies, has enlisted two associates (along with Redfeather's cousin and occasional tenant Simon desRosiers) for his personal attention to the project, according to Deputy William J. Moore, who is spearheading the operation.

"We have several prominent citizens here in The Creek," Deputy Moore told the *Creek Run* this morning, "and we were happy when Mr. desRosiers contacted us about Miss Redfeather's concerns. We took immediate action, and are happy to report that the property should be Silverized™ before Miss Redfeather returns from working on her current project."

According to the brochure issued by Hunter, the Silverize™ process is relatively simple but time-consuming. Based on the understanding that an active werewolf will immolate upon contact with even trace amounts of silver, fine strands of a secret Silverize™ compound are threaded around a property, through roof tiles, along outer walls and across windows. "These filaments are finer than the strands of a spider's web, yet will defend you and your loved ones from the most vicious intruder of them all," promises Adam S. Hunter Sr., president and owner of Silverize™ and Vortex Oil.

It remains unclear whether this signals a change of opinion on the part of Redfeather, who has always maintained a strong skepticism regarding the presence of werewolves in the area.

Said Hunter, "We are happy that a well-respected North American Native artist such as Karina Redfeather has chosen the original Silverize™ process to protect her home and property. Even in the unlikely event that she could escape an invasive attack, she would lose irreplaceable works of art, not to mention the damage inevitable to the house and its other contents."

Deputy Moore reports that two werewolves were spotted near Pigeon Creek this past week, though this is hotly disputed by Sheriff Langston, who denies their existence completely.

"Adam Hunter is the product of a Big Oil family who is trying to recoup industry losses by playing on ridiculous notions and creating a public panic," Langston said in a written statement issued today. "There is no more to these 'werewolf tales' than there ever was to *chupacabras* and Bigfoot sightings.

"Citizens of Pigeon Creek should go about their business and ignore the silver tongues, if you will pardon the pun, of modern-day snake-oil salesmen.

"The public should be aware that no member of Pigeon Creek law enforcement is affiliated with either Vortex or Silverize™, and that we will be conducting business as usual here at the Sheriff's Department."

Locals remain divided on the issue of werewolf existence. Janine Wallace and Shari Swenson, owners of the Pigeon Creek Diner and roommates in the old Morris house, are thrilled that the Hunters have arrived.

"It's time someone took this seriously," says Wallace. "Haven't you heard all the Bigfoot stories these days? We just wish we could afford to Silverize™ our big old place. I sleep with my great-grandmother's silver brooch under my pillow."

"We are so glad to have them here," adds Swenson. "In fact, now they're going to be here for a while, we would like to extend an invitation to stay with us at the Morris house instead of the motel. No charge, of course."

Karina Redfeather remains unreachable for comment.

###

Revenge of the Rina

Simon had prepared himself for Karina's fury upon her return. What he couldn't handle was her icy politeness. He thought he'd caught a break when she raged at nobody in particular that they had half their facts wrong; but then she asked him in her professional voice if he'd like more coffee. The kitchen had lost all its charm for Simon.

"That roof leak I was going to fix for you," he began. "I noticed when I was up there that you—"

"I didn't want to wait another month," Karina said, off-handedly. "I took care of it myself."

Offering to do any more home repair work, which she was perfectly capable of handling on her own, would worsen the strain between them. Simon tried a new tack. "I thought it was funny," he offered, "that your boyfriend got busted to meter maid for a week after that piece came out."

"Did you?" Karina asked absently.

"Rina."

"I'm sorry, I don't normally socialize with tenants. 'Family' or not. Excuse me, I have work to do."

Simon was left alone in the kitchen. The Silverizing process had taken three and a half weeks—a week longer than anticipated—due to a sudden late-spring sleet storm, and its day of completion coincided with a gathering of the press and Karina's return just the day before. The offending copy of the *Creek Run* lay on the table, badly crumpled at the sides.

He knew that the "cousin" pretense was compounding the problem, stinging Karina's feelings. But what else could he do? How would it look, he had explained, if he moved in to the main house and then took off and abandoned her in a month or two? Besides, it wasn't as if they would be seen having a life together. There was trouble brewing and he was there just to look out for her for a little while. Aside from all that, there was her reputation to think of. Karina's only response was to remind him what century it was and stalk away, wiping her eyes.

Simon sighed deeply and began pacing the kitchen, working out how to handle the next couple of weeks.

Gregory had immediately taken Old Jake off south somewhere, far from Vertigo's reach, while laughing himself sick over the idea that nothing would be more wildly dangerous than Karina when she came home from Duluth. He wished Simon luck. "Ain't no Silverizing against that woman," he chortled, and sent his love to her. "And I wouldn't advise you to try saying her name three times, either," he called from the road as he and Jake left to pick up the Greyhound bus from outside the diner.

There were two days left before the first night of the cycle, and Simon was spending part of them reviewing every strand of silver on the outside property, knowing that the house itself was already fully enveloped and impenetrable. "Take what you would have put on the guest house and use it on the main building," he suggested, and Deputy Moore leaped at that suggestion. So it was done. "Don't worry about me," he assured the red-faced lawman, "I'll just stay in the house with Rina on full moons." Not a soul had observed his skillful acquisition of enough threading to protect the sleeping area of his little cabin, internal door, windows and all, just in case he had to secure Karina in there, before the theft became too risky to continue.

The rest of the time he spent hunting Vertigo.

There were clear signs that the Firewolf King was still about, even though Greg had been prompt in removing Jake from the area. But why, Simon wondered, why would a Firewolf be in this area? If he'd been tracking Jake, they all would have known by now, or he'd have taken off south to pick up Greg's trail.

Rina was his first concern, as Vertigo's taste for torture often led him to women and small children. Simon shuddered at a twelve-year-old old memory of a summer's night in Texas, full of the screams of a mother and tiny child, and Vertigo's unbridled madness. It was the only time the two werewolves had come face to face. Simon had failed to stop the slaughter. They'd squared off, circling, when the lights came on in the rambling ranch house and a lone figure rushed toward them.

Streaking into the woods in opposite directions, the two werewolves barely escaped; but each now had the other's scent.

Thus, Vertigo had to be aware of Simon's presence and ought to have been concerned. Waterwolves were the thinkers, the planners who were not overtaken as completely as their fellows. Nobody wanted to be on the wrong side of a Waterwolf; even at Apex they were the intellectual masters and could hunt and kill any other of their kind.

Hunters. Of course. Vertigo was here for the Hunters.

In the next forty-eight hours, Simon had managed to patch things up a bit with Karina. With just a couple of days before the rise of the next cycle, he was nearly frantic for her safety. A new approach occurred to him, and he risked the whole Silverize argument again.

"It does work, you know," he ventured as Karina tore up yet another freshly posted "This property has been Silverized™" sign retrieved from the front of the long driveway.

"I don't want any of you dying because of me. I don't want you or Greg, if he comes back, or Jake, or anyone else thinking you hear a noise in this house and coming to save me and—I can't even say it."

"Then stay quiet the next five nights. Promise me that, Rina. Don't come outside. I'm not a pet."

She smiled and nodded, "I know, I know—'not behind the ears,'" and Simon exhaled. No more was said about the issue, and soon it was time for preparations.

"Remember when we met?" Karina asked on First Night as she heaped pre-sunset food onto Simon's plate.

She had been walking home from school, taking a shortcut through the woods on a snowy Duluth, Minnesota winter evening, when a small group of rough boys leaped out of the brush and pushed her into the snow. They chanted anti-Native slurs and scattered her books. The biggest one, an overgrown 13-year-old, began pushing her face into the snow. Someone else sat on her legs and she couldn't breathe. The snow packed into her mouth and up her nose. She couldn't hear a thing, and then suddenly she was able to turn her head and scream with all her might.

Then it all stopped.

The boys scattered and eleven-year-old Karina was helped to her feet by a tall, sandy-haired man in a long leather coat. He gently brushed the snow off her, gathered her books and asked if she was hurt. Rina thought he was the handsomest man she had ever, ever seen.

"Do you live far from here? No? I'll walk with you until you get home. You shouldn't take shortcuts through the woods," the man lectured, "you never know who you'll meet in here. Don't your parents tell you things like that?"

Karina nodded.

"You get along all right with your parents?"

"Oh, yes," Karina responded and chattered away as the man grew more agitated.

"We'd better go faster. It's getting dark."

"I love walking in the dark, especially under the full moon. It's my favorite thing to paint," and she talked on. Her companion seemed to be taking deep breaths of her, almost as if she were wearing perfume, and it made her feel quite grown up.

"My name is Simon, and you shouldn't talk to strangers," he said as they reached her house and he walked her up the steps, effectively ruining the little living fantasy she was having about being all grown up and arriving home with her knight in shining armor.

Simon knocked on the door, introduced himself and explained the situation. He declined the invitation to come in, and as he stood against the dimming light, Rina thought he had the kindest, warmest eyes she had ever seen. Unusual eyes with a slight ring of blue on the outer edge of the irises.

He saw her safely inside, and leaving her to an angry, part Russian, part Ojibwe, part English parental lecture that she didn't really hear, he disappeared into the woods.

Simon remembered this vividly. This innocent, confident child who had been kind to him during their conversation, who later that night lay safely sleeping under the moon as a shadow rose outside the window to fall over her quilt. The shape moved silently, and took form on the white coverlet, with a flattened crown and long hornlike ears. Simon shuddered.

"Time already?" asked Karina.

"I'd better go. And, Rina," he paused. "I mean it. I should

have told you about Vertigo and I'm sorry I didn't. Stay inside tonight, please. Remember that there's something else besides me out there. A true Firewolf." His voice was beginning to drop.

Karina looked into Simon's blue-ringed eyes and promised.

DINNER IN THE DINER

In the Pigeon Creek Diner, Janine and Shari were poring over the accounts and supplies books as they waited for the Hunters to come in for dinner. In spite of the sudden increase in tourists, few visitors had ventured in to the diner, most having arrived in their own well-stocked campers.

"This is disappointing, to say the least," sighed Janine. "When those UFO hunters were here, didn't we clear three thousand dollars?"

"Three and a little more over two weeks," agreed Shari. "I think we might lose some this time. Well, at least the Hunters are here."

Sure of their new regulars, the "Diner Ladies" had bought steaks to hold in reserve for the men as a "Hunter Special," and finally closed the books, deciding that even the local heroes weren't coming that night. They began chattering merrily about nothing in particular.

"The guys can eat at our house," suggested Shari, since the cars streaming past the diner suggested that yet again, nobody was going to stop there that night. "Where are they all going? I haven't seen this many cars since ... I don't even know."

"I heard they're all going to the Redfeather place, to look for werewolves and see if that Silverizing thing works," answered Janine as the diner's bells jingled. Both women leaped up to greet their Hunters, but instead their flirty grins disappeared when their lone customer skulked in. "Looks like that fella in here last month, only with teeth," shivered Janine. "Oh well. I guess he's mine."

"Your kids'll be actual redheads," Shari snickered and went to the kitchen.

The shabby figure seated himself near the door. He was lean and not very tall, with a scraggly reddish-brown beard that hid most of his features. His eyes peered through long greasy hair as if trying to read Janine's thoughts. She held her breath and handed him a menu from as far as she could reach.

"Is it always this quiet?" Vertigo asked with a slow and unsettling smile. This would be so easy. He was tingling with it already.

"Aw, everybody's out at the neighbor's place. She just got that silver thing done and everybody's waiting for werewolves to show up." Janine flinched as the man's long pinky nail scratched a jaggly V shape on her hand.

"Sorry," he grinned.

"What do you want to eat? We've got—"

"Just water."

Janine sulked her way back to the counter and made an ugly face at Shari, who grinned through the serving window. "He'll be a big tipper. Lucky you."

Vertigo sat back in the booth and gazed out the window. "Werewolves, huh? How many of 'em?"

"They say two, if there really are any."

Simon desRosiers, thought Vertigo, and the other fading scent was his little pet Jake's. There was a third as well, but he didn't recognize it. Never mind, he had two new toys to play with right here, and they had essentially fallen into his grimy lap. The younger one was pretty, he'd make her watch and take her second. Gear her up.

He saw the blood streak on the older one's hand. It was his own little game, to mark a V on his prey. He would wet his pinky finger first, to inject the wolf into them. It would never do to try this after sunset; new wolves bit hardest. He tasted the blood on his fingernail to reinforce the objective.

Janine brought the water. "Well, sir, we're going to shut down and go home before sunset. You know," she winked conspiratorially, "in case they're right."

"Why aren't you two over there?" asked the man, getting up as he drained the glass.

"Heck, we just live out back. Oh, no charge," Janine waved after him as he left.

Vertigo almost howled. *No charge? You've no idea what this is going to cost you.*

WOLF CIRCUS

Pacing in her front room, its window glass shimmering in the sunset from the fine silver threads, Karina was frantic. She was certain Simon hadn't had the time to get deep enough into the woods, and now the place was surrounded by Hunters and questionable press outlets. On her broad yard, there was even a huge gaggle of crypto-critter tourists who'd read the *Creek Run* piece, all of them crammed into an assortment of four-wheel-drive vehicles that they figured would outrun any problems—problems which they clearly hoped would show up.

"I hate this, I hate it," she fretted to Sheriff Langston, who waited with her inside until the sun had fully set.

"I'll call Bill in here and leave him with you," the sheriff offered, and at the same instant they both said, "Please" in very different tones.

Langston's eyes crinkled in amusement. "All right, all right. I hear he does well on porch duty." He picked up his hat. "I'm just here for crowd control, you know. Aside from that circus, nothing is out there. You do know that?"

Karina nodded but kept pacing. "Thank you, Sheriff. I wish

you could make them all go away."

"They'll tire of it when nothing happens. Where's your cousin?"

"Manning the guest house against souvenir hunters."

"That's good, that's good. I wouldn't worry, though. Even the Marines couldn't get in here tonight." Langston stepped toward the front door, hesitating before placing his hat on his head. "Well, see you in the morning, Miss Redfeather. I'll be here if you need anything. Hope you can get some sleep."

Karina thanked him and closed the door against the flashing lights and the gawking masses. Her heartbeat started to slow as she realized that Simon was correct—in wolf form, he would avoid this mob with their tripod torches and smartphone pitchforks. Perhaps, in the strangest of ways, they would actually protect him.

By three in the morning, most of the crowd had quit tossing emptied plastic beer cups onto the property, turned off their headlights, and finished having their pictures taken with the Hunters, who were loving every moment of it. Adam was the possible exception, moving from glamorous square-jawed superhero to moody, pacing Hunter, his eyes shifting from log cabin to woods, occasionally pausing to listen intently. Bill, stuck on trash-pickup duty, wasn't as happy as he would have liked to be. A few hours later, shortly after sunrise, Karina saw a small light flicker inside Simon's log cabin and knew he had come home.

The die-hards wouldn't leave for some time, until the

weather got the better of them at last. It was a drizzly gray morning, and the mostly hungover crowd dispersed up Karina's long dirt driveway to line up in front of the diner up the main road. Sheriff Langston pulled up to his office down the street, puzzled as to why the ladies hadn't opened up for such a large clientele. It was after 8:30 already.

He radioed Bill that he was going to check on the "Diner Ladies," and walked across the parking lot behind the little restaurant. The door to the old Morris house was ajar, so he hopped up the steps and pushed it open.

Sheriff Langston had spent his postwar career at the scenes of car wrecks and house fires, and had seen more than his share of Army horrors. This morning, he took a large step backwards, tripped off the porch and threw up.

MOON OF THE HUNTER

By 9:30 a.m., Sheriff Langston was being treated for shock on the way to the hospital, and law enforcement—such as it was in the form of Bill Moore and the Hunters—was taking charge of the proceedings. Karina's property was invaded by all two members of the Pigeon Creek press, and everybody with a badge, a patch, or a pen seemed to be looking for Simon.

A few terrified neighbors dropped by seeking company and to discuss the previous night's horrors. For all the isolation of Pigeon Creek, nobody could remember similar tales of a madman on the loose. And the dear Diner Ladies, of all people, they whispered. It wasn't as if they were the sort that would materialize at the truck station and disappear into the night with who knew whom.

"What do they mean by 'werewolves?'" someone asked. "I thought they just made that up as a term for psycho killers."

"Who cares what you call it? I certainly don't," added another, "because we're getting out this afternoon. Hell, most of the town is leaving."

In the meantime, the Hunters gathered on the porch, followed by an assortment of odd amateur Web reporters holding up phones and a wide range of other portable video devices.

"I did not see desRosiers last night!" Deputy Moore declared meaningfully, and several times, to anyone within earshot. The three Hunters leaned against the porch railing and trained their eyes on Karina, daring her to make up excuses, as she appeared on the doorstep.

"I've told you, he spent the night protecting the guest house, where he lives, from the actual lunatics." Karina held her front door open for the Whitehead family, whose trio of small children carried teddy bears and blankets into the house.

A slight noise rustled near the porch, and Simon appeared. "I saw *you*," he informed Bill, "at about three o'clock in the morning, trying to coax phone numbers out of tipsy coeds outside my window."

The Hunters grinned and Karina went cold. Simon winked at her but his eyes were serious. He quietly asked her to take all her guests inside the house, leaned toward Adam and handed him a piece of cloth, speaking barely audibly. "I'd get dogs in if I were you. Guess you know Howler Sign when you see it?" Adam nodded and slowly stood up straight from his leaning post. *Dogs won't track Howlers, and I'll bet desRosiers knows it. What's his game here?*

"Come on then," Simon continued. "I'll take you out there and show you his base. Karina," he called inside, "what do you say to a neighborhood sleepover? I don't think that many locals are staying behind."

In fact, those few residents who were not yet ready to leave town were only too happy to stay at Karina's well-protected house, whether they believed in werewolves or not. Karina was able to take in the Whiteheads and another local family, the Hillstroms, along with a young tourist couple, the Chos, whom Sheriff Langston had sent her way when the Pigeon Creek motel shut down. They all arrived bearing personal supplies and enough food to sustain the group over the next few days and nights. It was a tight squeeze, but she offered the Chos her bedroom, the Hillstrom family the living room and the Whiteheads the bright, airy studio. All the other locals had simply left town, leaving behind the morbid thrill-seeking reporters and a large gang of lookie-loos. Everybody in Pigeon Creek had known and liked the Diner Ladies, and the silence in town had a tangibility to it.

A legitimate TV reporter finally arrived from Duluth with his team and was shouting questions as the Hunters disappeared with Simon into the woods.

"Follow them or talk to me," Bill thumbed his chest and ordered the news crew; for once, Karina was glad of his distractive presence. She went into the living room to settle people into the welcoming, overstuffed furniture there. Not surprisingly, everyone was quite happy to squeeze in next to the warmth and comfort of someone else they knew. Karina reminded the group that they would be fine moving around and even going outside until dark, at least as long as Bill was protecting them. There was a nervous giggle at that, but nobody moved. Karina turned on the television, which sprang to life with an image of her own front porch.

"And we are here live with Acting Sheriff William Moore. Sheriff Moore, what else can you add to what we have heard already?"

"This is definitely the work of werewolves. All you skeptics out there, listen up. Two of these things have been spotted in the area so take the proper precautions. You don't," he turned directly to the camera, "repeat, you do not know who your neighbors are here."

Everybody groaned and then laughed heartily for the first time. "Do I know you?" became the afternoon's catch phrase, along with observations like "I'd pass the bread if I knew you," and then finally, when the cameras moved toward the edge of the woods, the adults let the kids out on the porch for some supervised fresh air. Just one brief moment clouded the gathering, when the TV announcer droned on professionally about the possibility of two werewolves, and everyone shot glances at the Chos.

"Hah, you actually don't know us, do you? We can go," began Tony, gently taking his wife's hand and placing it on his knee, but the entire group except for Karina was blushing, and the group patched everything up with apologies and some light humor before the conversation turned to what information they all knew so far.

"What do you think about last night?" ventured Lara

Whitehead, and a hushed, sometimes quietly tearful discussion followed. Whether it was a maniac or a made-up monster was irrelevant; it was not going to be safe in Pigeon Creek until either the Hunters or Bill Moore caught him. The unanimous vote was that the Hunters stay, but the guests' opinions on leaving town remained divided.

"No, please stay here," Karina insisted as others offered to move on. "There are crowds of people around here now, even if they are a bit morbid. And the Hunters have to be some help no matter what kind of psycho is out there. Nothing is going to get in here, and nobody weird will come near the place," she smiled, and turned away into the kitchen before they saw the fear in her eyes.

Simon must have spent the night in the guest house, right under their noses after all. How he could have maintained control was beyond her, and she picked up a nearly empty coffee can. It seemed that her very own house had become headquarters for all the activity. The neighbors chipped in with the food they had brought along, feeding and watering the ghoulish crowds who'd driven in from afar. Each gawking visitor seemed to be hoping for an appearance by werewolves, if not the "escaped lunatics" of childhood campfire tales.

"They're saying werewolves! It's not werewolves," scoffed a professorial type who gratefully accepted some hot tea. "It's extraterrestrials. Nobody will tell you that, though."

Karina spent the next few hours passing out water and hot drinks to the people outside, keeping her personal houseguests in good spirits, face-painting the Whitehead children and giving them paper and colored pencils to play with.

Simon was in a foul mood when he returned after leaving the Hunters camped in their heavy vehicles to catch up on sleep.

"Do you have to feed all of Minnesota?" he growled, trudging up the steps and elbowing an annoyed Bill out of the way. Karina stifled her snappish reply when she realized that Simon hadn't seen the sun properly for all the drizzle and his time deep in the woods that day.

"Are you going to stay in the guest house again tonight?" she asked quietly once they were alone in the kitchen.

"No." Simon leaned against the counter and grinned in the way that always took her heart. "I almost blew it last night when your boyfriend was talking to those college girls. I wanted to smash out the window and give him something to arrest," he laughed. "So no, tonight will be worse, and then tomorrow is Apex. I'm not coming near this place." He peeked into the living room, its occupants gathered near the fire, and shivered slightly in his leather jacket. "Rina, I don't want to be overheard. Come over to the guest house and listen to me."

They strolled past the last of the crowd. Chased off by Adam's gang, the ghouls had dispersed into their vehicles and were leaving as the afternoon threatened to draw to an early, stormy close. Soon only Bill and the Hunters remained around the grounds.

Once they'd reached his quarters, Simon spoke quickly,

warning her to stay inside the main house no matter what she saw or heard.

"I know exactly where the silver threads are," he explained, "but Vertigo will find it harder to sense them. I can leap the ones on the perimeter, because I installed them so I could come close to the house if I needed to. Vertigo knows the risk and might not chance it. And if it comes down to a battle between me and Vertigo, Rina honey, even I will not recognize the people I know and care about." He raised his eyes, "I'll just take out everybody within range, and so will he. And for now, keep me happy, will you? Stop feeding the masses unless they have a reason to be here."

Rina reached over to brush the hair from Simon's forehead and his heart stopped. He gripped her forearm until it hurt, staring at her wrist. "How the hell did that happen?" he demanded hoarsely, staring at the V-shaped nick that bled ever so slightly.

CRASH AND BURN

Simon's irises were beginning to edge with pale blue.

Karina glanced at the clock; it was too early for this to be happening. Simon's fingers gripped her so tightly that she almost couldn't feel her hand.

"Remember." Simon's voice dropped and it terrified her.

"I do—I do remember him. He was raggedy, he just wanted water and—he kept staring. He was a little strange, but there were so many people around that I wasn't worried about it. *Simon. You're morphing.*"

"I'm not." Simon released her and looked away. "That was Vertigo. He's marked you. Rina, for God's sake, come back to the house with me now, and gather every piece of silver you can."

"It's all in the safe deposit box," she reminded him.

"Stay away from the windows, then, at least, so he can't identify you by sight. Dammit, he'll scent you, though. I'll let the Hunters know. Maybe your boyfriend will guard the porch again but we're going to give him something useful to do. GO!"

Karina's hands fumbled the door latch, and she turned to

pour all her emotions into him silently.

Simon returned her look yet didn't seem to see her properly. He was morphing, she was sure of it, and as he shuddered, he hissed, "I feel him; run NOW!"

"I love you!" she wanted to scream, as if she'd never get the chance again, but instead backed away and ran to the main house. "I think Simon is coming to talk to you," she called to the Hunters as she ran across the now-empty grounds and up the steps, gathering her guests into the cottage for a lockdown. How odd it felt, explaining quietly to the adults that Simon might have seen something, and that a madman might be planning an attack.

Everyone was surprisingly calm, and Karina watched the Hunters leap into action, Simon shading his eyes and hunching while pointing out the likely avenues of assault.

Run, Simon, run now! What terrified Karina most was not Vertigo but Adam. He had to suspect the truth, as Bill did, and from the living room window she could see the look on the Hunter's face as those suspicions grew. Simon was hunched over, ostensibly searching the ground, refusing to meet Adam's icy gaze.

Suddenly, Simon shot a look at the window, and was gratified to see the curtain drop and the glass darkened by a blind. Fine threads of silver glinted in the dull light, and he flinched. He turned back to see Adam's half-smile and the satisfaction it betrayed.

"You know a lot about this," Adam observed.

"So do you," snarled Simon quietly as he headed rapidly for the woods.

The Rush was coming early, and he couldn't hold it off as well as usual. Vertigo had to be close by, triggering the intensity, but Simon couldn't scent him. He was already well into the woods, running much faster than humanly possible, and for the sake of covering his own tracks, refrained from pulling off his jacket and sweater. The shoes had to go and went soaring high into the treetops; he figured his jeans were probably not going to survive the night but kept them on. The adrenalin began to flow, and Simon felt the familiar tingling between his shoulder blades.

His hands began to lengthen uncomfortably, and he noticed, startled, that they were beginning to take on the more wolflike shape of Apex rather than Second Night. My god, he wasn't far enough into the woods and he couldn't be near people … oh, Rina … but it didn't matter, as the tingling crept up his spine to his jaws, his vision dulled and then sprang back into sharpness. His ripped clothing was restrictive and frustrating in the extreme; what was left he shredded off himself with his razor claws, snarling, tearing it to bits and chewing the pieces like the lunatic he'd become.

And there! Simon smelled Vertigo and threw back his head, howling long and hard, streaking into the new darkness after his prey.

The Firewolf had been tracking him; within seconds they were on top of one another. Their shrieks and howls reached the house, to set the patrolling Hunters on edge and the company inside, horror-stricken, huddling together. Outside, Bill suddenly needed yet another pair of trousers.

"There!" Adam's blood was up now, and he sent an armed and grateful Bill to the porch to stay out of trouble. "Don't wander off too far, now, Bill," he laughed after the toddling Acting Sheriff. "Once you hear that charming blend of Harley Davidson and fire siren, it's too late to run!"

He turned quickly to his Hunters. "That's two of them, all right. Well boys, we'll get to see how Silverizing works in a few minutes," and he laughed again. His companions aimed their rifles at the direction of the rapidly approaching howls and found they could not breathe.

Two rifles fired and missed as the werewolves, one golden-yellow and one black, hurled out of the woods and straight for Adam. Bill screamed as the yellow one, without stopping, took the head clean off Travis Figueroa and aimed itself right at the deputy.

Only Adam's howl of rage was louder as Bill screamed again, spun around twice, shouldered open the door and launched himself into the crowded living room with the two beasts at his heels. Both creatures had easily leaped the Silverized porch and landed neatly inside, squarely on the carpet, Immediately, a third silver shot, not even close, splattered high on the living room wall. Outside, two guns reloaded, and the screams inside the cottage wouldn't stop.

Just as the yellow wolf Vertigo lunged at Karina, the panic-stricken Bill slipped in front of it and fell to its fangs.

He lost his humanity in a heartbeat.

Sickened, Karina saw the instant change as Bill, whirling in agony, became a yellow beast, howling with newborn rage. The creature she knew as Simon fell on top of the other two and sank his teeth into Vertigo, and all three werewolves rolled and howled in a tangled mess of teeth and claws away from the humans and toward the kitchen.

Three things happened. Adam Hunter stepped across the threshold, simultaneously kneeling and firing a silver bullet that hit Bill, immolating him; Vertigo sank his teeth into Simon and then hurled himself over Adam's head, out the door and onto the lawn to make his escape; and then Simon turned on the crowded room, snarling, dripping, advancing. The children shrieked, but the adults could only grab them and hold them close, trying to place themselves in between their offspring and the black werewolf.

Adam fumbled his next bullet and the beast, sensing the silver, avoided him and lunged for Rob Whitehead.

"Simon!" Rina screamed and threw herself into its path, "Simon! Simon!" she sobbed the third call, and the werewolf stopped. It lowered its head, slavering, closing in, just inches from her, snarling low and long. Not even Adam could move.

Then it was gone.

GOOD MORNING TO YOU, TOO.

"**D**on't move," Adam ordered, redundantly.

The group huddled in Karina's living room stared at the quickly fading spot of ash that was once Bill Moore. Adam trained his rifle on Karina and his left hand still fumbled with a bullet.

"Don't," Karina began, "No …"

Adam took a large step forward and lowered the gun. "Don't move," he repeated. "That thing dribbled on you. You have a cut there." Karina jerked back and Adam snapped the rifle up. "You have a cut on your hand! It drooled on you and it's not sunrise yet! *Do not move your hand!*"

There was a collective gasp as Adam stepped forward with the silver bullet in his outstretched hand. "You there, Reese?" His surviving colleague stepped into the house. "Stand ready, then—"

Adam broke off and turned on Karina as Reese leveled the rifle at her—"*I said do not move.*"

Karina now felt the werewolf's saliva on her hand, edging toward the open, V-shaped cut left by Vertigo the day before. She was too shocked to think. Adam reached out to her with the silver bullet.

"This could hurt, Miss Redfeather," and as he tapped the silver against her wet hand, the skin surface burst into a phosphorous flash. Her hand was now dry.

"Did that sting?" Adam stepped closer. "No? Any other cuts? Sure? Let's check," and he ran the bullet gently over her exposed skin. Several small flashes erupted. His eyes met Karina's and she was taken aback by the compassion she saw there.

"Let's decontaminate," Adam spoke to the group, as Reese turned to the door, standing half in, half out.

"They're probably gone now," Reese checked the distance, "but let's stay put until after sunrise."

Each person stepped forward to allow Adam to run the silver bullet check, the little ones curling into their parents' shoulders and squeezing their eyes shut. The only other flashes, very small ones, were found on Rob.

Adam suggested that the group disperse into the studio and kitchen, while he detained Karina and sat her on the sofa. The Chos, who had begun whispering together, shot Karina an accusing look before leaving for the bedroom.

Adam sat down next to her, but was quiet for a moment. Then he smiled slowly. "I wasn't sure if that was going to work."

"The bullet thing?"

"Yes. It was a shot in the dark—uh—so to speak. From what I could see, you had seconds left."

Karina looked intently at the Hunter. His customary arrogance was absent as he continued. "You might have been an unusual blend of Firewolf and Waterwolf."

Ah, he was testing her.

"Not sure what you mean?" she countered.

"You know exactly what I mean. You called desRosiers' name three times."

Karina put her head in her hands, genuinely exhausted. "I don't know where he is. I was calling him—he's my cousin! What if the werewolf got him?" Would such a red herring work on this man, she wondered.

"You've been harboring a werewolf." Adam was surprised at the shock in her eyes. Could she really not have known? But … "You called him three times," he repeated.

"I don't remember anything except wanting to find him."

"Well … not surprising, I guess. Simon is your cousin? Lives in the guest house, around sometimes, gone others?"

"He does a lot of construction and logging work, so it all depends on the season. I hadn't seen him in years, until a couple of months ago."

"The ladies at the diner met him only once, and I find that odd."

Karina looked blank. "Why is that odd? Simon lived *here*, he ate *here*."

"They knew you."

Karina hid her face again. "Everybody knows me. They've collected some of my art, and there aren't many other women—why am I even explaining this to you?"

"Why do you think Simon went into the diner with his friend last month? Casing the place, maybe?"

Adam had her full attention again. "Oh, you can't possibly think Simon was involved!"

So, she wasn't denying it. He tried another angle, "It could have been his buddy, that old toothless tramp he was hanging around with there. Those murders had all the marks of a Firewolf."

"But—"

"Listen, Miss Redfeather. We know that crazy vagrant's a Firewolf, because we've been tracking him. It's a short step to think that Simon desRosiers is the Waterwolf that was spotted with him. And you can dispense with the 'cousin' farce as well."

Karina finally started to shake. "Who is the animal here?" she demanded. "Bill Moore died on my floor! He's …" she indicated the only remaining relic of the deputy—his badge, which had been torn off and now lay half under the carpet.

Adam hesitated in his interrogation. Her distress was real enough, but there would not be much time to get more out of her with all that had to be done before Apex tonight.

Reese called in, "Sunrise," and the cottage came to life again suddenly.

The Chos couldn't get out of the house fast enough, still shooting angry looks at the red-eyed Karina. The Hillstroms weren't far behind, after leaving their contact information with

Adam.

"Who the hell will believe us, though?" demanded Mr. Hillstrom, ushering his wife out the door.

"We hope that now everyone will, Sir."

"You," Tony shouted at Karina as he entered a Hunter vehicle, "You are messed up! You and your—" he made air quotes through the vehicle's half-open window, "friends!"

Adam stood up. "Don't jump to conclusions, now." Karina stared at him.

"Yeah." "Right." The pair locked the van doors and Reese sped them out of sight.

Rob Whitehead was more sympathetic. "You saved my life. You risked everything for me and for my family. I can't thank you enough." His wife chimed in but the children were still terror-stricken. The family had gathered their belongings, and by this time Adam was on the phone speaking quietly to who knew whom.

The children's wide-eyed silence was somehow as terrifying as the attack. Karina couldn't take her own eyes from them as her heart broke.

"Yes, look at them," Adam said softly over Karina's shoulder as he pocketed his phone. "This is what you are condoning when you support Howlers."

Karina turned to him. "I don't know what to do about Bill," she waved a shaking hand toward the badge on the floor but couldn't look at it.

"We'll take care of it after my team is through here," Adam

extracted his phone again and began punching numbers into it as he moved outside.

Karina stared back at the Whiteheads. "Is everyone ... I don't know what to say. I don't even know if you want to stay."

"Safest thing is to get out of town," suggested Adam from the porch, "and stay away for now. And for the kids' sake, get them out the back door, if you have one." He'd blocked the front entryway with his own tall frame. For the first time, Karina saw through the window the decapitated Hunter lying in the dark rain. She let the drape fall and tried not to vomit.

Adam saw her face and nodded, speaking quietly to her again. "You ought to feel sick. That's who he really is. You aren't doing anyone any favors by protecting Simon desRosiers."

"Go away," Karina finally broke down and sobbed. "Leave me alone."

"Honey," Lara Whitehead put an arm around Karina and drew her into the kitchen with the rest of her family. "We can stay if you like."

Karina shook her head, "The Hunters are right. You should be taking the kids as far from here as you can." Lara gave her another hug and then gathered the whimpering children and their toys close to her.

"I've never talked about this," began Rob as he hoisted his bag to his shoulder, "but we think my uncle was taken by a werewolf, decades ago now. I remember Uncle Carl; he used to come around even after the rumors started, and then suddenly we didn't see him anymore. We kids missed him; it was …"

The kitchen door opened quietly, and they all stood up straight. Simon was there in the half-light, casting an odd shadow over the table. "Karina," he held his hand out and spoke softly, "I need to see you right away." He nodded to the Whiteheads, tossed his dry jacket over Karina's head and shoulders, and spirited her out into the rain.

Adam spotted them from the front steps. *Oh, I will leave you alone, then.* Turning away coldly, he began forming his next moves. *If you happen to see the news tomorrow, desRosiers, you will be surprised at first, and then relieved. But I will come for you anyway, monster, and then you will find out what 'alone' feels like.*

At the same moment, Lara stared at the closing kitchen door. "Should we …?"

"I don't think so." Rob took a deep breath and sat back in his chair. "No. No, she'll be all right. Let's just go."

Many minutes passed while the Whiteheads remained silent. Something about the appearance of desRosiers that morning was nearly as terrifying as the apparitions of the previous night.

The Creek Run—Werewolves Attack Pigeon Creek, Artist Redfeather Disappears

Pigeon Creek—The community suffered terrible losses this week under the apparent attack of at least two werewolves, possibly three.

First came the horrific murders of our beloved Diner Ladies, Janine and Shari. They were brutally assaulted and dismembered the night that the rest of the community was assembled at the property of artist Karina Redfeather, whose property had just been through the Silverize™ process. No witnesses have come forward related to these murders.

Last night, in what seems to have been a coordinated attack by the creatures, Acting Sheriff William J. Moore and Hunter team member Travis Figueroa were killed at the home of Redfeather, who seems to have disappeared early today, after these most recent murders. She was last seen in the company of Simon desRosiers, her cousin and tenant.

Adam Hunter, founder of the Hunters group and heir to the Silverize™ and Vortex Oil fortunes, spoke with the *Creek Run* early this morning. He and surviving associate Reese McConnell wore black ribbons across their silver patches.

"We are deeply saddened by both the loss of our teammate Travis Figueroa and the death of Deputy Moore," Hunter stated. "We are now working with authorities to locate Miss Karina Redfeather. She was taken from her home this morning allegedly by Simon desRosiers, who is currently a prime suspect in the murders of this week. Our objective is to bring home Miss Redfeather before tonight's full moon."

Accounts of the events differ. Mr. and Mrs. Tony Cho, visiting from Duluth for a getaway, insist that one of the werewolves was in fact Mr. desRosiers, a claim disputed by Rob Whitehead, who was also present during the attacks and who also says that Redfeather left of her own accord with desRosiers. Adam Hunter will neither confirm nor deny this rumor, stating only that his team is now working to find both Redfeather and desRosiers.

Meanwhile, Sheriff Langston remains under observation at Red River Hospital and is not expected to return to duty any time soon.

###

WEREMEN

Simon wasn't himself yet.

He'd taken Karina's hand, though he was distracted and distant, and with a start she felt the faint traces of hair on his palm. He didn't meet her eyes, instead pulling her across the wooded property to the guest house. Karina struggled to match his pace.

"Could you slow down a little? I feel as if I'm being kidnapped."

That drew a look, and sure enough, he wasn't fully back yet. How strongly was the presence of Vertigo affecting him? And Old Jake, what effect would his bitewolf, Vertigo, have on him if he were around? Heaven help Jake and anyone who got near him.

The early morning was silent except for their footsteps as Simon half-dragged her onto the porch and through the guest house door.

"You can let go now, Simon." Karina stated as they entered the chilly living room, her hand still in his grip. "Simon." His shoulders hunched, Simon averted his gaze and mumbled something unintelligible, shaking visibly.

"Simon!"

He turned and bathed her in a wide-eyed stare that took her breath away. He shook off the night, breathing deeply. Karina shivered a little. Third time, indeed. "Won't the Hunters be coming for us?"

"Probably. They must know where you are, but last night I left them …" Simon paused to gauge how squeamish she might be after the previous night, "… I left them a good long trail of half-eaten deer leading north and into the deep brush, so they'll follow that first. We have a little time, but not enough to relax." His voice was still husky. "The others will be here soon. Greg and the rest, I mean."

"With what 'rest'? With Jake?" Karina heard her own voice rise.

Simon bent to start a fire in the wood stove and waited silently until the flames took hold.

"Simon??"

"We'll be out of your hair before Adam and his goons come knocking on the door. Don't answer it and you won't be able to tell them anything."

Karina sank into an armchair, kicking off her wet shoes, tucking her feet under herself and hugging a large cushion.

In a few minutes, she was able to force a laugh. "All right, so I've been kidnapped into my own guest house. Why? To feed me to our scary friends when they get here?"

Simon sat down on a bench next to the crackling stove, ignoring her jest. "There's more that you need to know. For a start, this is where Greg and everybody else will be staying this week."

"Everybody? Wait, who's 'everybody'?"

"Things are moving quickly. More of us are coming."

"Things? What things? And who is everyone that's staying here?" Karina looked around the small, well-furnished room, envisioning it in tatters within a few days.

"When Greg gets in we'll talk. 'Everyone' is our guys, for the moment anyway." Simon pulled a soft throw blanket from behind him and stepped over to place it around Karina's shoulders. She drew in the warmth he had lent it.

Simon was pacing now. "As soon as I knew Vertigo was around, and I knew you wouldn't leave, I called a meeting of the pack, right here. We all agreed I ought to bring you here for a chat because there are things you need to know."

He spoke with a little less gentleness than was his habit. "I wanted to keep you away from your guests, all of them. It'll be a little while before the Hunters wake up and come over here. Stay out of sight. Then—"

Without warning, she sprang from the couch, propelling herself into his arms, and he breathed her in as she clung to him, shaking. Sometimes she smelled the way she did when she was just a child. She had the scent of innocence, of loyalty and the hint of another, tied to a promise made long ago. He forced away other emotions that had begun to haunt him very recently.

"Bill; and that Hunter," was all she could manage.

"I know. Shhhh. Shhhhh," he held her loosely, wondering where to begin what he had to say next. Instead, he reminded her that they'd be meeting up with Gregory, Old Jake and the others any minute. "We don't have a lot of time before they get here. I've pepper sprayed the grounds, here and at the main house," he continued. "The gang is not too far away. I've got the kitchen stocked for them so if you want to grab a shower while I get breakfast ready, go ahead. Oh, and yesterday I raided your closet and packed you a bag with fresh clothes and everything in case we really do need to get you out of here. It's in the bedroom."

Karina tried to penetrate Simon's thoughts. She shook her head slowly and pulled away. "I blew it. I called your name last night. I'm sorry. I'm so sorry."

He gave her shoulder a quick squeeze but ignored her apology. "You'll be shaky for a while. You understand now why I said to stay put? It doesn't matter that I didn't hurt you last night. Tonight is Apex and you must stay still and quiet right here inside the guest house, not at home. I don't want you leaving here. There's a whole gang of us around, with more coming who don't know you, or your scent, at all. And Vertigo wants you."

"I hate to ask this, I really do. But if it's such a problem, shouldn't I be safer inside my own house with the goon squad that's taken over my porch? And with that Silverized thing all over it?"

Simon shook his head. "I've actually pepper sprayed all

over this place, and Silverized the bedroom section, which is where you are going to stay hidden. Vertigo thinks you're in the main house, but Greg and I will guard this place; and the others are going to try and lead the Hunters off the grounds tonight."

"The Hunters are a man down, though, Simon. Will they really follow the others? Won't they just stay at the house?"

"I don't know, but that's not the critical part. Just remember that none of the other wolves except Vertigo will come after anyone inside a house, unless that person is attracting attention.

"Vertigo's the only one who would go after static prey, and right now, for him, that's you. He knows that your place is Silverized, but he's had time to plan now. He could probably still make a run for you now that he's seen inside and has a feel for where the threads are. So stay put here. I'll put word out that you're staying here with me and that the Hunters are protecting the grounds. If Vertigo comes, and I doubt he will, he'll likely get himself immolated." He continued sharply, "And besides, I don't like the idea of Adam Hunter using you as bait."

"And that's not what you're doing? I can't tell what you're up to. You look like a—like some kind of lunatic."

"You've seen me look worse." Simon took a few paces around the room and stopped at the window, facing the rising sun.

Karina took a verbal stab at her old friend. "Stay here,

alone with you—whatever will the neighbors think!"

Simon ignored her. "How's your new project going?"

"The hanging scroll mural? It's all right, I suppose. I don't know; I don't really feel it as much. It's … something about the fact that it's just supposed to hang there. I like working on solid things."

Simon nodded, and when he turned to her, the blue rings had gone completely. He spoke gently now. "Maybe you need things in your life to be a bit more stable."

Karina wanted to argue but she was too tired. She headed instead for the shower, but even after twenty minutes, she couldn't wash the night off. She brushed her teeth but ended up retching into the sink and had to start over. Too exhausted for a private, cleansing cry, she disappeared into the bedroom to curl up and think. She'd wrapped herself in one of Simon's sweaters when she heard Greg's quiet arrival and caught fragments of a low conversation that included phrases like "taking a nap," "How did you convince her," and "They're all coming. Already. It'll be big," before the voices dropped to an inaudible range.

In the kitchen, the two men were preparing a vat of chili to ward off the coming night's ravenous appetites.

"Not too many beans, there, Simon; nothing worse than a flatulent werewolf," Karina heard Greg's warning jest, and Simon chuckled in spite of himself. "Aroooooothhhhppttt," followed by laughter was the last thing Karina heard before burrowing into the pillow in disgust, and finally drifting into a fitful doze.

Greg, meanwhile, broke into a more serious vein. "She would be a lot safer at the main house, you know."

"He can't trace her here."

"Who? Vertigo or Adam?"

"Both," Simon viciously decapitated an onion.

One by one, the others arrived and gathered in the small kitchen, some of them observing the scent of pepper spray. "Some of it must have leaked," agreed Simon. "It doesn't take much. I can't scent any of you, either. Burns like blazes."

Gregory produced a small bottle of hot sauce for his sizeable meal, "But never enough," he grinned, "never enough."

After a while, Karina reappeared, fresh and lovely as if this were an ordinary getaway, and was introduced to the group. Tyler was fairly new; he was a forestry grad student who had run into wolf trouble six months before and was still acclimating to it all. Karina hugged the delighted Old Jake and was introduced to Carl.

"By any chance, are you Carl Whitehead?" asked Karina, and Carl nodded. "I think I might know your family."

"You do, yes. I like to stick within a couple of hundred miles and keep an eye on them and see who's around," Carl said shyly. "Or I stay even closer, sometimes. You never really know what's out there."

"Which seems to be the prevailing feeling," observed Karina.

"Well," Carl could hardly look at Simon, "if things can

happen to guys like me, or like Simon …"

"Carl was my bitewolf more than eighty years ago, and he's not over it yet," laughed Simon.

"I'm just so sorry," Carl offered quietly. "Simon was there changing a tire on the road, and I was just a new guy. And …"

Gregory finished, "And he looked so *tasteeeeeeeeeeee.*"

The entire group erupted in laughter, and that was a good thing for all around. It was a relief for Karina and Simon, a bonding moment for the wolf-men, and the very cloak needed for a shabby russet mess to detach himself from the guest house roof and skulk off into the woods.

Apex

Simon stopped just short of tucking her in just before sunset. "If you don't leave me alone soon I'll bite *you*, and heaven knows what you'll turn into tonight," Karina teased, "skipping through the woods every month with ribbons in your hair, wielding paintbrushes and a teddy bear." He'd checked the blackout curtains for shards of light. The bed took up most of the small room, and he cautioned her to stay on the inner edge, away from the Silverized window.

"Go," she prompted gently, noting the early onset of the blue rings. Simon pressed his forehead to hers, inhaling deeply, and left.

There was only silence outside, and the hours dragged on. Karina was dozing off lightly by midnight, but her tumbling thoughts had drifted into a nightmare that was intensifying. She was home but not home, Simon had gone, and the whole stone cottage was sparkling in a spider web full of flaming, shrieking werewolves. She kept running from room to room, window to window, calling their names, trying to save them all and unable to stop each tortured demise. Then she heard it, the snuffling, scratching noise just outside the window, and a howl just inches from her left ear.

Another shriek, and a wet claw smashing through the cabin bedroom's tiny window brought her fully awake. Golden-yellow death with five spiked claws dripping saliva searched the mattress, trying to scratch her, to turn her shape.

Karina spent three or four seconds scrambling out of the way, unable to vocalize, looking for a place to hide, until it became clear that this beast had been unaffected by the Silverizing and was going to get in.

She screamed, an unbidden primal sound that echoed through the woods, and she didn't care if it brought Adam Hunter. This was not Old Jake, it couldn't be; the group surely had him well under control deep in the forest.

Her next shriek was as wild as the wet claws that snatched at her and barely missed. It was coming in.

Karina wished for anything silver, anything to throw at this raging beast. Was it one of Simon's friends, or was it Vertigo? How had he found her? In the next second the bedraggled, hairy clawed arm was retracted and a hellish ruckus began outside as other wolves howled in.

She was gasping and couldn't stop, yet her mind began to settle.

Suddenly, with the eerie clarity of the mortally threatened, she was calm, and crouching on the floor by the far side of the mattress, stared at the vicious scene through the torn curtain and shattered glass.

Though it was difficult to see it all, nothing could prepare any human for what was outside. Old Jake was indeed there, manic, foaming, snapping at Vertigo's tail with his monthly set of fresh fangs. It was either Simon or Carl who stood tall, long arms raised, waiting for the instant to strike and howling like a banshee. A smaller black wolf, Tyler most likely, circled the pack. Greg, the huge brown Earthwolf, was now engaging Vertigo face to face, snarl for snarl, in an earsplitting shriek battle, each lunging for the other's throat.

Where was the other black wolf? Where were the Hunters? How could they not hear? Was Simon still there? And in tune with that last thought, the black brush outside the window moved. There was an eye in it. The blue-ringed eye engaged Karina's and narrowed. She didn't even hear the snarl, but recoiled and dived under the bed, praying he hadn't seen the movement, trying to buy time. *Oh, don't let him try to get in—he'll be immolated.*

The battle raged on, though nothing was trying to get inside now. She spent a heart-pounding few seconds coming to terms with her situation—oh God, please, what if one was already inside through the living room? They'd touch the bedroom door, they'd be destroyed. Names, quick, remember the names, but it was pitch dark inside, and how would she know them only by their glowing eyes?

It didn't seem close to sunup. Where were the Hunters, she thought with a cramp of guilt.

The screams and howls of the wolves must be audible for miles. There was no way she would risk another peek out the window; even Simon would find his rage toward her unchained this night.

There was a lull in the noise. Karina hardly breathed as she moved out from under the bed and pressed her ear against the bedroom door. What if one had got in? Would she be able to hear it?

Suddenly, again the screams outside were overwhelming. It was impossible to think that one Firewolf could hold off so many others, but Vertigo must indeed be supernaturally powerful, and thoroughly demented. From time to time, horrific sounds indicated possible wounds.

The night would not end.

A final long, high-pitched shriek and it all suddenly stopped. Karina's ears rang.

Then the growls picked up, low and slow and long. They came closer to the guest house, closer, and Karina wished with a sickly giggle that she had some pepper spray. Adam Hunter's words haunted her, "This is who he really is."

Was the dawn coming?

She heard the click of the front door. Oh my god, they were in. Karina sank to the floor, back against the bedroom door, and waited for death—her own or that of an immolated wolf or two. She rested her head on her knees. She could save the first one, whoever he was, and be turned with a bite, just by opening the door so he wouldn't touch it. Although, then they might both be immolated, or the whole pack might kill her. She couldn't think straight, and something dragged closer,

closer. It stopped short of the Silverized bedroom door. There was a faint light in the room. The sound was strange, now, a huffing, painful one. It moaned, and the floor shuddered, and shuddered again. A half-howling groan, and the whole nightmare stopped.

Sunrise had come.

THE SPILL

Karina felt the door shake slightly and heard whoever had been on the other side move away. The guesthouse door clicked open and several footfalls padded their way into the brightening world.

She stood somewhat shakily, cracked open the door and peeked down the hall, seeing her five shirtless and somewhat tattered friends, still slightly hunched and wild-looking, gathering by the kitchen. Nobody spoke, but Simon looked over his shoulder, tried to smile, and approached her carefully as she opened the door wide. "Are you hurt?" he asked quietly, then for the first time in their long friendship, he held onto her until she felt she couldn't breathe. Karina had wanted Simon to hold her that way since the moment she'd met him.

But suddenly, Old Jake was crying. His sobs were muffled but came from the depths of his soul, so that Karina moved quickly to soothe him and reassure him that she was unhurt. Activity began then, as Jake was settled enough to take a shower, Greg got breakfast started and the night's madness was recounted.

"Save Tyler and me some bacon and fill us in later," Carl

said from the doorway. "We're going to track Vertigo. We'll come back after the Hunters have left. They ought to be here at the guest house soon." Simon wanted to go, too, but Gregory held him back.

"Need your ears on this, before they come around to investigate. I'll sneak off when we hear them coming." Greg motioned Simon and Karina to the kitchen table. Jake was now tucked into the living room sofa and slept fitfully there.

"Karina," began Gregory, "give us any detail you have, anything at all. There's no way Vertigo should have got past that Silverizing." He turned to Simon, "Unless … that whole thing is a scam?"

"Doubt it," responded Simon wearily. "It tingled like silver when I had it done—"

"I thought you couldn't be affected by silver unless you'd morphed!" Karina interjected.

Gregory stared at both of them. "Don't you tell her *any-thing*?"

"I tell her enough! Rina, details. Where were you situated exactly, and …" he saw the deep hurt again. "For God's sake, I am just trying to protect you!"

"It's not working." Karina stated.

"No," agreed Gregory, but he hadn't taken his eyes off Simon. "It isn't working. And Simon, how the hell did you get so close to the wall?"

"I don't know. I really don't know. My hands and arms were—I'm all slippery. Huh." He stood to examine himself and turned to Karina. "What do you remember?"

After a moment, Karina answered. "I was on the bed, toward the inner edge where you told me to stay. Not against the wall, anyway. I heard the howling …" she shivered.

"Yeah, he does that. Likes to plant the terror before you see him." Greg nodded.

"Then this dripping wet arm came right through the window, and it started clawing."

"Wet? It looked wet to you?" Simon stood up straight, rubbed his hands together and smelled them.

"Yes, it was dripping."

The two men locked eyes. "It couldn't be that simple," said Greg, taking a whiff of Simon's fingers. "Lord almighty." They both stood up and headed for the bedroom. The sheets were ripped and oddly stained, fabric and foam exploding from deep furrows where the mattress was shredded. Simon bent over and inhaled deeply, then muttered explosively in language Karina had never heard him use.

"Is it motor oil?" Greg took the sheet from Simon. "I'll be damned."

"He drenched himself in motor oil," Simon explained to Karina. "He literally slipped right through the Silverizing. My god," he paused, "he must have been lurking around the place the whole time, listening. The pepper spray must have covered his scent."

"Take Karina back to the main house," ordered Greg.

"Back to Silverizing and Adam Hunter? They won't protect

her as well as I can! I took care of her perfectly well last night!" Greg silenced him with a combative stare.

"Where the hell are those Hunters, anyway?" Greg growled \. "Wonder what the holdup is. Simon, if you and Rina don't get back to the house before they get here, and Rina doesn't say she left willingly, you are going to have more than Adam Hunter, the law, and Vertigo to contend with." Karina had never seen Greg look so menacing.

"I'm going to check things out." Simon stormed through the hallway and out the door.

"So … Vertigo really rubbed motor oil on himself?" Karina asked Greg.

"Poured it all over himself, more likely. Maybe even bathed in it. We should find a pile of empty cans outside. Lucky break for Simon—he got it on his paws and arms. Saved him when he reached the wall. Sorry." The look from Karina worried him.

They joined Simon outside to find him talking with Tyler and Carl. Their eyes were watering. "Here." Simon held up one of several large punctured cans.

"Holy—" began Greg and jerked away, as the scent of pepper spray overwhelmed his nostrils. "*Ugh!*" It was strong enough to catch Karina's full attention as well.

"Well, that's covered his tracks. We'll never find him. I'm betting he'll be back tonight, though," Carl stepped back. "I've got to get away from this. Come on, Ty, let's see if we can't find something, at least. We'll be back in the afternoon unless we have anything to report sooner." The two headed off into the woods.

"Simon," Karina whispered as she jogged up to match her friend's long step, "are you saying you retain some werewolf aspects even when you haven't morphed? That you should have scented Vertigo?"

"I heard that," Greg called out from the front door. "Simon! We three are having a little chat right now! Meet you at the table. I just want to check something out here."

Karina and Simon reentered the guest house in silence. Karina couldn't bring herself to ask anything, but Simon glanced at her occasionally as he set to brewing a large pot of coffee. "Obviously," he admitted slowly as Gregory stepped inside, "I have not told you everything."

"Obviously not," Greg observed darkly.

"It was the best way to protect you. If anyone ever asked you about werewolves, you wouldn't know the answers, or you'd give the mythology, and they wouldn't connect you to me as an accessory."

Greg stated what was already on Karina's tongue, "You were protecting yourself."

"How can you say that!" Simon exploded. "The less Rina knows, the better! Especially with those Hunters around!"

"Hunters have been around only for the past century or so, that we know of anyway. We've been around for millennia. Sit."

An angry silence surrounded the table. Karina was

stunned: a whole century of Hunters? What was going on here?

"I thought you two were a couple!" Greg's tone had not changed, and Rina looked as if she'd been slapped. "No?"

"We've been friends for about fifteen years or so," Simon responded defensively, "and there is no need to complicate things"—he could have bitten off his own tongue—"with details that would involve Rina more than she already is."

At that moment, Simon would have traded Greg's glowering expression and the fathomless pain in Rina's eyes for a Hunter's bullet.

"Go on," Greg ordered, tapping the table. "Let's hear it. All of it. Now."

The Truth, Sort Of

The sounds of coffee being sipped finally chewed on Greg's last nerve. After a deep breath or two, he finally exhaled, "All right, Karina, fill me in from the start. How did you and Simon meet?"

Karina's gaze left her mug to focus like a laser on Simon, then drifted to Greg. "He saved me from some kids who were ganging up on me after school."

Greg nodded.

"He walked me home, because it was winter and almost dark. I remember his eyes ..." Karina trailed off.

"It was full moon?"

"Yes."

"You saw him turning?"

"No," Karina tipped her mug back and forth in one hand, and with the other, ran her finger through the wet ring it had left on the table.

"Aaaannd?"

"Well, that was all. He brought me home, talked to my parents and then left."

Greg gave her a long look. "And when did you see him

again?"

"Not for a few weeks."

Greg turned to Simon. "And when did you see Karina again?"

Simon uncrossed his stretched legs and recrossed them. "I guess in a few weeks." He flushed slightly, and Karina noted that Greg had inhaled quietly, deeply, in the same way that Simon had as he walked her home to her parents. The men's eyes met.

"Later that night." Simon's frame hunched over, Karina stared at him and Greg nodded again.

"So you were marked." Greg watched Karina as he spoke. "And that's truth number one."

Karina shook her head and slumped in her hard-backed chair. "Marked," she murmured.

Simon looked up and into Karina's eyes with an almost pleading gaze. "I took in your scent. If we met again, I would always know you, no matter what my form might be."

"So you would never hurt me?"

"I still could. But the marking, the imprinting, helps protect you against that—"

"Or makes her prey," boomed Greg.

"It's a tool," breathed Simon dangerously. "Vertigo uses it differently."

"A tool—wait, so you are saying you actually have me marked the same way as Vertigo—"

"Why do you think I got you out of your house last

night?!"

"So, this 'marked' thing," Karina felt as if she were running full speed toward an open ledge, high above a canyon, "what does it do to your feelings? If it's just a tool, I mean." The canyon ledge drew closer.

"Truth," declared Greg.

"Nothing," responded Simon, very softly, looking into her eyes, and the log-cabin walls shattered all around her heart. There seemed to be wind, cold, unforgiving, rushing past her ears and she could hear and sense nothing. That awful word, "Nothing."

An eerie moment stretched on, filled with nothing.

"Karina, you know how I feel about you," Simon began.

"I don't think she does."

Karina's breathing was shallow. "I'm what, a pet? A toy like Jake? What?"

"No, come on. Rina. After all this time."

But in all this time, Karina finally acknowledged, he had held her only as a sister, had never kissed her the way she'd wanted, and never would. She had hoped, all this time, that he was just waiting for her to be old enough—because he was what age, now? Seven human years to every wolf year, so he looked late thirties, but was bitten seventy-some years ago, so—oh, it didn't matter—but in fifteen years, hadn't she grown into him? Had he not known there was nobody else and that there never would be?

"How did you not know?" Karina choked. "How could

you!"

Simon turned pleading eyes to Greg, whose stony return glare showed him no mercy.

"Rina … I was looking out for you." His heel tapped the floor. "Rina, you know exactly how I feel about you. We've had this conversation! When did I ever …"

"Next truth." Greg's voice was like distant thunder.

"There's more?" Karina pulled her knees up to her chin and wrapped her arms around her ankles, curled there on the hard chair, staring at Simon.

"I'm just beginning to understand this one myself," Greg declared, "and I think Simon knows more than he's letting on. So, Simon," Greg leaned back, folding his wrists behind his head, "the Fourth Bloodline."

"Nobody knows."

"May I remind you that I have several decades on you, most of them spent in the Crescent City?" Simon flinched at that, and Greg went on, trying to lighten things for Karina's sake. "N'Awlins will teach you to spot a lie whether you can smell it or not." But the joke fell softly onto the floor.

"Simon," Greg continued, "if I am not mistaken—and I know more about this than you think—you are among the few who actually know the truth about the Fourth." Again, Greg tapped a strong finger on the table. "I hate to ask you, more than you know, for Rina's sake. But for her sake, I *am* asking you. When was your last contact?"

Simon leaned on both arms and gave Greg a level look. "A

few years ago. The fourth line is strong. And they have our backs, particularly against the Hunters. More than you think."

"That's not what I meant." The vestige of lupine wildness tinged both men's demeanors, and Karina suddenly recognized the permanence of their condition.

"A few years ago," Greg insisted. "So are you or are you not still in touch, more or less?"

"Not ... exactly."

"You're hedging. You still keep up with her?"

Karina felt a kick to her heart. Of course. Of course. Why would Simon not have a lover, and of course she would be like him. "I'm going home," she declared and stood up.

"I'll walk back with you," Greg's voice was powerfully compassionate.

"That's fine. I'll be fine going back on my own. Besides, I couldn't explain why you were with me."

"Don't be ridiculous—I'll walk you back!" exploded Simon.

Greg rose as well. "I'll give you two a moment. I'm sorry, Rina."

Simon was at her side and brushed her hand. "I do care about you, Rina. Can you understand that?"

"Not really," she responded tonelessly, withdrawing her hand and her heart into the growing light of day, fully seeing the sun.

MY LITTLE RUNAWAY

Greg had blocked the cabin doorway with his own frame when Karina left, and she could hear the two men arguing almost until she reached the edge of the long drive to her own house. She hesitated, hiking her bag up on her shoulder and digging one foot into the dirt. The cool pine-forest air smelled refreshing after the night's onslaught of pepper spray, blood, and beast.

Karina wheeled to follow a light sound behind her.

"Hello, Miss Redfeather," Adam Hunter stepped out of the woods and onto the dirt road. "Good to see you are safely home. Of course, you weren't too far away, were you." His tone was friendly, and he held out an arm to her but returned her cold stare. "Come on, I'll walk you back."

"I can manage."

"Where are your friends?"

"There's just Simon. He figured I'd be safer away from you and your crowd." Karina's heart began to speed up. "Is there any particular reason you feel you have the right to interrogate me on my way home?"

"Oh," Adam's eyes slid across to hers. "An immolated

deputy, a decapitated colleague, several terrified residents, and a helluva racket in the woods last night. If there had been more than two of us left, we'd have put an end to it. There are more of us today, though," his grin was as wildly wolfish as anything she's seen the previous night.

"I'm going home. Why don't you move along and leave my property? I imagine I'll be safe for, gosh, another month without your help, thank you."

"No, you won't."

Karina would have happily clocked him with her bag but didn't quite have the energy. She shot Adam a look that tolerated no argument, and focused her unrelenting gaze at him.

"You've been crying! Whoa," Adam stepped back with a glint in his eye as Karina swung the bag from one shoulder to the other, just missing him after all, and took off at a stride.

"Well, excuse my Texas manners, Ma'am, but I'd be happy to carry that for you while you tell me all about it." He kept pace with her, goading. "Tough night?"

"When I get to my door I want you gone. I'm calling the police."

"The police. Really? Well, honey," drawled Adam, "who do you think might be available now?"

"Whoever picks up the phone."

"The fact is—Ma'am—that we are all you have here at present." He matched her long steps as the cottage came into view.

Karina stopped short. "My house."

"Yes, Ma'am."

"My house. Who are all these—what are you doing with my house!" Despite her exhaustion, Karina broke into a fast trot, the bag banging her hip with every step.

Large vehicles, from campers to SUVs to cars, surrounded the cottage, with Hunters moving about the yard, the porch, even inside. And … was that a federal government vehicle?

"This is a big deal now, Miss Redfeather. Your house is a crime scene, of course. With all those witnesses, you'll find that the Feds are finally taking the existence of werewolves seriously. We're getting all the evidence and help we need."

Karina was barely listening. "I want those cars off my lawn. I want everybody gone."

"Should I tell the Feds you said 'get off my lawn'? They'd love to hear it from you personally."

Karina tried to shake Adam off as he pulled her aside into the trees. "In fifty more feet, they will know you are here."

"Good! I want to go home."

"If you do, I'll be making some phone calls and you will be talking to a whole lot of fascinating people who won't be half as charming as I am. You'll come with me so we can talk privately. I'll get you something to eat; then I'll bring you back here in a few hours. Or if you want," he was close enough that she could hear his whisper, "I can just take you back to the guest house where all your furry friends are, the ones that nobody knows about—yet." Bingo. He had her.

Adam drew her back up toward the main road, sticking to the overgrown bushes paralleling the long drive. They moved quickly, reaching a small, nondescript car hidden just off the highway. Adam wrestled her bag from her and tossed it easily over the back seat as he held the door for her. "Don't try and run; if you start any trouble, you'll be the one telling stories all day and night."

Fine, Karina thought, but just wait until we get out of town. "So, you don't figure on being followed?"

"Me? No," grinned Adam, pulling out onto the highway. "Everybody reckons you've been kidnapped, but then, everybody is looking for desRosiers, aren't they?"

Karina sank into the car seat.

"Talk to me, Miss Redfeather. We can work this out so that very few people get hurt."

"As opposed to?"

"As opposed to more people like Travis, the Whitehead kids, and Bill. And no, it does not matter that Deputy Moore was a yellow-livered toad." Adam was tight-lipped but shook his head. "You still don't see it."

Karina was silent.

Adam glanced at her. "Or maybe you do, finally. Want to tell me about what happened last night?"

"There's nothing to say."

"Yet." Adam stepped on the gas and said no more. And the hours-long stalemate had begun, with a brief and silent stop at a roadside stand for food and other needs. Karina's mind began to form a way out.

Once night had fallen, along with a couple of inches of hard rain, they were still on the road. Adam had stuck to routes off the main highway. "I'm not taking you home until you talk to me," he warned, but Karina still wasn't cooperating.

"Hungry?" Adam's voice reached through the thoughts tumbling around in Karina's mind and she shook her head.

"We won't be stopping anywhere for a couple more hours."

"I'd like some water if you have any."

Adam reached into the compartment between the two front seats. "It's not cold, sorry."

"It's all right, thanks." Karina's heart began racing.

Inside the compartment, tucked under the water bottle where Adam hadn't noticed it, was her getaway ticket. Now, for a reason to pull over and get at it.

If she could get out at a gas station and locate an old landline phone, there might be a chance to call her grandmother. It had been so long, though—how would her grandmother take such a phone call? They hadn't seen each other since Karina was about five. Her grandmother hadn't even attended her own son's funeral—it had been eight years, Karina remembered sorely, since her father's sudden death.

"I'll need to stop at the next place with a restroom," she announced.

"All right."

Twenty minutes later, they rolled into a dully lit, muddy way station. The rain had eased to a smatter, and Adam caught her by the wrist as she reached into the back for her bag.

"Going somewhere else?" he smiled with no warmth.

"Girl things. I need my bag."

Adam raised an eyebrow.

"I told you, it's a girl thing. I'll ruin your car seat," she declared and he released her. Thank heaven that for all their blood-and-guts bravado, men were awfully squeamish about certain kinds of biological events.

It was just about that time, though, and she hoped Simon had remembered her calendar and found what she was going to want when he'd packed her things. It would be just like him to take care of her needs like that. She pushed that thought away, and Adam caught the flicker of pain.

"We'll be there soon," he said gently. "I promise, you will be safe and cozy. And fed."

"I'll be just a minute," Karina murmured, and disappeared into the convenience store for a bathroom key. Once inside the restroom, she checked the bag, found that Simon had indeed left her with everything she'd need for a few days on her own, and then stepped back to size up the tiny window. She'd never break through those vents. Maybe she could wait this out …

And she did, ever so coolly, thinking and waiting.

Eventually Adam came knocking on the door.

"I feel sick," Karina told him in muffled tones. "Could you do me a favor please? Could you get me some painkillers?"

"We'll be where we're going soon. Come on out of there; the sooner you do, the sooner we'll be there."

"I can't … cramps …" Karina forced a retching sound as she turned on the faucet to a convincing splatter in the sink. "Adam …"

She heard a muffled groan as he stepped quickly away. "I'll leave the car open." He turned the corner into the store.

Well, if she couldn't pull this off, at least she had her bag, and she ducked into the night, hidden from the clerk and Adam as they navigated their way through the puzzlement of painkillers for women's ills.

Yet again, Simon had taught her a skill she'd laughed about at the time. "You live by yourself, and you never know." She swiftly entered the car, found the basic tool kit in the compartment where the water bottle had been, and began sweating her way through the process of hot wiring the car. Her fingers were numb but Simon had made her go over it and over it, finally making her repeat the whole procedure in the dark, "because that's when you'll probably need to do it."

The store bell dinged just as Karina crossed the wires and gunned the gas; Adam jumped after her, grabbed the handle and jerked the door open, but Karina wheeled the car and he slipped off, yelling something she couldn't catch. *Well*, she thought, laughing silently, *who are you going to tell?* and tore off into the night.

Karina was very familiar with this road. She knew that the terrifying beauty of the wild bush country led to hikers going missing and becoming disoriented in the dense brush, only to be located, far too late, mere yards from a roadway or lake. For Karina, though, it would be excellent cover.

Dammit, though. The car was now dangerously low on gas; Adam must have wanted to get to their destination and not use his credit card at the station. Karina pulled into a recess off the paved roadway as soon as she could and began covering the car with branches and other growth. She raked and scuffed the tire tracks on the shoulder, settled back into the car, and began to doze in the darkness under the gentle rain.

Shortly before dawn came a brutal *crack* on the branches. Bewildered, Karina came around sharply and stared through the windshield into the enraged eyes of the man she'd fled the night before. The window broke on the passenger side; a gray sleeve punched through, opened the door and revealed itself to belong to Adam's companion Reese, the youthful red-haired Hunter who was now leaning into the car and motioning her out. There was no choice. Karina grabbed her bag, exited the vehicle as commanded and stared the men down.

"We're Hunters," explained Adam, coldly. "Remember?"

That Lonesome Thing

Carl and Tyler had returned to the guest house mid-afternoon with foul news; they'd found evidence of having been followed to the main cottage, possibly by Hunters, and absolutely no trace of Vertigo.

"It gets worse," Carl intoned as the group huddled in the galley kitchen. "Adam Hunter was waiting for Karina at the drive and wouldn't let her walk on by herself. I doubled back to see what else was going on; the place is full of Hunters. There's even an FBI van there. Looks as if they're using Karina's house as a base. She'll never be able to leave on her own."

"How do we get her out?" asked Tyler, shrugging off his jacket. "Hey, Simon—she wouldn't say anything, though, would she?"

The parting expression on Karina's face was imprinted on Simon's conscience. "No, I don't think so."

"She looked pretty upset when she was walking toward her house," observed Tyler. "You sure?"

"Pretty sure. She wasn't mad at you."

"We're busted, though," Greg's voice was low. "At the risk

of sounding like a bad movie, we'd better split."

Old Jake was going to be a problem. Attached to Simon as he was, and sensing Simon's fear for Karina, he could not control himself, and began babbling and rocking on the living room floor.

"I've got him," Greg nodded. "Carl, Ty, you want to split up?" Both men shook their heads. "Ty's still new," explained Carl, "and we don't know what's coming."

Simon put his coffee mug down forcefully. "I'm going after Rina."

"You'll never get near the house," warned Greg.

"You'd be surprised."

"Yes, I would. Shocked." Greg leaned his back on the pantry door and crossed his arms. "Look, Simon. If Karina had been mad enough to talk, they would have this place corralled already. My guess is she's buying us some time. Let's take it." He held up his hand, "And before you go charging in like a white knight, ask yourself how that would look. It makes Karina an accessory to murder, at best, if you confirm all those suspicions. At least this way she can claim she never knew anything. Just the way you wanted it."

Admitting that fact was painful. Simon nodded silently.

Greg waved his hand around the galley, "Ty and Carl still have bikes, but the rest of us, we're going to have to travel the old-fashioned way."

"The train again?" asked Tyler, hoping for a safe place to stow his mountain bike before jumping into a moving freight car.

"Hope you still have your harmonica," muttered Simon.

"Can we sing? Can we sing?" clapped Jake, looking up hopefully from his tucked-up spot on the floor, eyes still wet.

"Just not in public," Carl came into view, his bag packed to bursting. "Remember what happened to that opera tenor, what's his name—Lorenzo—three or four months ago?"

"What happened?" asked Tyler.

"The Hunters started an ugly rumor that werewolves are uncannily good singers, particularly good at harmonizing."

"Actually," broke in Simon bleakly, "that one is true."

After a pause, Carl continued, "Well, after one particularly good show featuring a particularly striking duet, a group of Hunters was waiting for the poor fellow at the stage door. The commotion nearly ruined his career."

"What!" exclaimed Simon, the world having regained his full attention.

"Huh," said Tyler, "so that's what my cousin meant when my aunt broke up his garage band."

"Let's just go." Simon stood up suddenly. Everybody had packed and was more or less ready to leave.

"I'll take care of Jake. We'll meet at the train." Greg rose with a grin. "Where do you want to head?"

"Not far, I'd say. South Dakota, Nebraska maybe?" Carl's voice came from the porch as he scouted the surroundings.

"Not nearly that far," Greg shook his head vehemently. "We really aren't myths anymore so it doesn't matter where we go; there's no point in hiding for long. Adam Hunter's crowd will attract everyone who's ever seen a werewolf movie, and I'm gonna bet that on our end, we have the biggest wolf gathering in history next moon. If Vertigo's here, he's probably summoned the rest of the Firewolves. I want to see what their angle will be."

"Outside Duluth, then?" Simon looked up from the duffel bag he was cramming with extra cans of food.

"That's far enough, yeah. That should do it. Somewhere northeast of the city, say ..." Greg was tracing a foldout map now, "right here."

Simon hesitated a moment, recognizing the territory. He met Greg's steady gaze, which carried a warning to keep silent.

"And we're gone," Greg declared. "See you all at the train." With that, he and Old Jake headed south into the woods; Carl and Tyler biked west; and Simon, fully aware that Greg would know his every move no matter what he did, struck out east, backtracked anyway and began to hunt the Hunter.

The rain grew steadily heavier. Simon, while preserving as much of his previous night's wolflike self as he could by sticking to the deep shadows of late afternoon, was frustrated by the confusion of olfactory leads in the woods. He could hear the movements of many people tromping on the porch and snapping twigs around the house, but Adam's scent remained the most recent in the drive, along with Karina's. It looked as if Hunter had taken her himself, and driven off. Think, think.

He felt Greg before he heard the quiet voice. "Let it go, Simon."

When he turned to face his friend, Greg simply said, "Even if Vertigo is following her, she'll be safer in there with Adam Hunter's crowd than with us," he jerked his head toward the dirt road as his eyes bored into Simon's. "Given everything, she's actually better off with him alone right now."

For the first time, Simon felt the rain, the cold, the absolute defeat of the day, and the emptiness of all his unspoken words. Every icy raindrop stung his skin. His bones were devoid of marrow. It was all too late.

"Come on," Greg said gently. "Nothing more you can do here. Let's go. Come on, I promised Jake we'd take a real train tonight."

Within a few hours, the odd trio had joined their companions aboard a freight car and begun the soggy, dark journey, Greg's harmonica echoing the mournful whistle in the lonesome night.

Local Artist Now Subject of Manhunt

Pigeon Creek—Missing artist Karina Redfeather is now the subject of a Federal manhunt, as is her cousin Simon desRosiers, according to an FBI spokesperson (who wished to remain anonymous as he or she was unauthorized to speak to the press) in a phone conversation this morning.

After a second apparently wild-sounding night, which occurred this time with no reports of personal or property damage, what's left of Pigeon Creek's edgy population awoke to the sight of government vehicles throughout the town, concentrated on the Redfeather property.

Rumors say that the howls heard in the woods belonged to several different individuals, but guesses as to the number are hard to come by.

The Whitehead family, who had been staying at the Silverized main house, were allowed to leave late this morning and spoke with the *Creek Run* on their way to Duluth this afternoon.

"We were startled when Simon took Karina away with him, but I wouldn't call it a kidnapping," states Mr. Carl Whitehead. Mrs. Whitehead agrees, pointing out that there was never any animosity evident between the two. "Beyond that, we are not supposed to talk to the press about it," she said, adding, "Actually, we were not supposed to talk to you at all."

The couple and their small children proceeded on their way, but not before the Whiteheads mentioned that Adam Hunter, leader of the now-famous Hunters, was also missing. "Who knows where?" was the only response they could give.

Adam Hunter was indeed unavailable for comment today, and no further information is forthcoming.

Editorial note: The print edition of the Creek Run *has been suspended for the time being, but the* Run *will still be available in its online format until further notice.*

MARKED

Karina's escape, while invigorating, was short-lived and enough to put her in Adam's bad books again. His interrogations grew colder as the group waited inside the car for a Hunter vehicle to appear with a can of gas.

"We're turning around," Adam informed the SUV's gray-clad driver, and the two vehicles headed back toward what the Hunters kept referring to as HQ. He turned to Karina, who was ensconced in the back seat. "Let me point out to you, Ma'am," oh, she was tired of hearing that voice, "that if you were to do something silly like call the police or the FBI, why, you would have to explain every little thing to them."

"Like the fact that I was kidnapped by UFO hunters? I'm not worried about the FBI."

"You ought to be. Because, Ma'am?" Adam's iced smile had the intended effect. "Where do you think we get our equipment?"

The rain was again pounding on the roof of Karina's cottage, which was surrounded by Hunters, nearly all of them men.

They seemed frighteningly self-sustaining, Karina noted in the brief look she'd had in the darkness as Adam and Reese hurried her inside.

There was no trace of the violence that had occurred there in the living room, where Bill's immolated self had left not a scorch on the wooden floor. Karina wondered how the Hunters might have handled the solitary badge but couldn't bring herself to ask.

Adam "allowed" her to go to her room, which nettled her to distraction. She stood there for a moment, fighting the feelings of illness that had plagued her all day. After a quick shower, she was able to pull on some loose jeans and an oversized sweatshirt that read "Resisting Invaders Since 1492," drag herself into the living room, and curl up on the sofa, wrapped in a soft tartan blanket.

Reese McConnell's red hair caught the firelight from the river rock hearth. "It was a good try," he offered a bright grin along with the steaming mint tea he presented to Karina. He had the same Texas drawl and outdoorsy good looks, but none of Adam's understated swagger. "Hot wiring a man's car. You really kicked him in the … uh, guts."

Karina accepted the hot drink and drew the blanket closer around her. Reese continued, "Funny as hell, though. Who'd a' thought?" He sat down on the large padded rocking chair next to the sofa.

Karina managed a watery smile through the steam above her mug.

"Aw, he'll get over it." Reese shook his head and chuckled, rocking gently.

"I'm quite sure he will."

"You're not hurt or nothin'?"

"It's just been a bad day or so, thanks."

"Yeah, I guess. Adam said you almost got bit? One of 'em marked you or something?"

Karina had almost forgotten. She looked at the red V, which seemed unusually fresh, on her hand.

"Here, lemme see that, can I?" Reese leaned toward her and gently took her hand. "Shoot, that's Vertigo's mark."

"There are other marks?" Karina stared at him and then caught Adam's eye as he came in from the cold soggy night. There was an air of pepper spray about him.

"Others?—Hey there, Adam—others, hell yes. All the Firewolves mark their vics if they can. Kind of a—trademark, I guess you could say."

Adam shed his gray jacket and nodded to Karina. "Sorry about getting you carsick."

"This is helping, thanks." She raised her mug to him. "Sorry about the back seat."

"Can't be helped. Thought you were pulling another fast one." Adam stood with his back to the fire. "You are just determined to get killed by a Howler, aren't you? Do you want to know what he did to those diner ladies first, before he killed them very slowly? Because I'll tell you."

"Hey, now, Adam," Reese looked slightly shocked. "I think

the lady can guess."

Karina's look said it all, as the flash of a dripping gold claw came into her vision, seeking, slashing.

Reese took the tipping mug from her hands. "That's enough, Adam, come on now." He turned back to Karina. "That Howler won't get to you here. There's a dozen of us, heck. And to bring you back, we backtracked, crossed tracks, sprayed, oh sorry."

The green tinge was returning to Karina's cheeks.

Adam picked the lecture up, "I mean this, Miss Redfeather. I've been after Vertigo for years. Many years. He doesn't wait for the moon. He's out there, and he's coming for you, either as mad wolf or maniac human. He'll keep you and …"

Reese looked at her sympathetically.

Adam continued, "Look. Sounds like your cousin is a decent guy, at heart. But the wolf has his soul now, and it will just get worse."

To her horror, Karina began, "But you're wrong! It isn't like that," but caught herself and managed, "But you're wrong, about Simon; he isn't what you're saying. He's not a … werewolf."

"Honey," Adam sat down next to her. "I'm exhausted. You're exhausted. Your cousin's a werewolf." *And I'll be damned if he's really your cousin*, he thought.

Watching Karina, Reese stood up and changed the subject. "All this pepper spray makes me want some hot chili. You up for that yet, Ma'am?"

"No, thanks, Reese. I'll be fine by tomorrow, though."

Adam's ice-blue eyes looked almost straight through her. "Careful, there, McConnell, the sweeter she is, the closer she is to jacking your car."

Reese flashed a broad smile on his way to the kitchen. "You must be plotting all the time, then, Ma'am."

It was difficult to dislike Reese, in spite of the silver patch, the gleaming bullets in his belt and the wolf's ears he carried.

So she turned her attention to Adam. "I hear the only way to kill one is to immolate it."

"Pretty much, yes."

"So is that why there's no evidence that they exist?"

"Yep, pretty much."

"No trace at all?"

"Never has been."

"So … those wolf ears are pretty much an affectation, then? Pretty much?"

Adam leaned in close. "I swear. I am going. To feed you. To that thing. When it gets here."

"Well," sighed Karina, sweetly, "then I hope all your back-tracking, crossing, spraying and cleaning out the back of your fancy vehicle was worth it."

She called a cheery good night to Reese as she strolled into the bedroom, plotting her next move with a ferocity that might have startled even Vertigo.

Through the long night, as he tossed on the sofa, Adam tried to imagine Karina as an ugly old maid. It didn't help. She

was probably going to be one of those coolly elegant octoge-
narians with scorching eyes, the sort of woman who
uncovered your soul and painted it onto your own skin as a
canvas.

He threw a cushion and beaned McConnell, who was snor-
ing loudly in his sleeping bag in front of the fire, and listened
for any similar rasping sounds that might emanate from the
bedroom. Nope. She evidently slept like an angel.

He tried to stop thinking about what she was wearing in
there, focusing instead on the rancid task she'd left him in the
back seat of the car. She honestly hadn't meant to, though, and
her distress was undeniable. He'd sent her inside with Reese,
battling the urge to hold her until the trembling stopped.

Well, this was useless. Even though the place was moni-
tored, trap-rigged, Silverized and alarmed, even though there
were ten other trained Hunters camped out on the property,
with Vertigo on the loose—in any shape—Adam was going to
be happier trusting his own senses. He got up grumpily,
huddled under a poncho and went out to sit on the porch with
his rifle until dawn.

In the morning, Karina awoke to the comforting scent of
brewing French roast, though for an unsettled moment, could
not recall where she was. She dressed as quickly as she could,
and startled Reese in the hallway near her bedroom door with
a mug of coffee in his hand.

"Oh! Well, good morning, Ma'am. Coffee?" He stepped
back into the living room and placed the mug on the long table

in front of the sofa, next to what appeared to be half of a chocolate bar. "I thought you might want a little chocolate this morning," he began shyly, and went to retrieve his own coffee from the kitchen.

"Thank you," Karina smiled, "a little chocolate never goes wrong."

Reese grinned, "There you go plotting again, I guess."

"Where's Adam?" Karina twisted and scanned the room.

"Outside. I reckon he'll take care of Vertigo when he gets here. One of us will," he shook his head, grimly. "This is kinda Hunter HQ now."

Karina counted on fixing that little problem soon enough, and nibbled the dark cocoa bar. "Thanks for this."

"Oh, well … my sisters—I've got all sisters—I know that's what they want if they—when they—at that time of—"

"It's perfect," Karina rescued him, smiling. "Exactly what I needed."

"Forgot about that until I was half-finished," Reese added, his blush fading.

"How many sisters do you have?" Karina studied the young Hunter. He might be about five years younger than she, enough to feel the need to call her Ma'am, she supposed.

"Well, now …" Reese said softly. "Well, Ma'am, I had three. But there's just two now."

"Oh, Reese, I am sorry."

"Ma'am."

They were quiet for a moment, listening to the birds' delight in the new, wet morning.

"Ma'am?"

Karina sipped her coffee and nodded encouragement. He was really sweet, this kid. How on earth did he get mixed up with the Hunters?

"It was Vertigo, Ma'am."

"Sorry, what?"

"Vertigo took her. She was our little sister, just fourteen, and—"

"Oh, Reese. Oh, Reese, I am so sorry."

"I'm gonna get him; I am, you know. I'm gonna tear that—"

They jumped as the door opened to Adam, who shook off his poncho and walked silently to the kitchen.

Presently he returned, his own large dose of caffeine in hand. He nodded to Karina and reminded Reese that it was his watch. A watch was superfluous, the two men knew, but it gave them something to do.

Adam gave it a try. "Have you eaten yet? Eggs sound good? Even with chocolate?"

Who are you and when were you sprinkled with pixie dust, Karina wondered.

"Look," Adam explained, "we are all going to be here for a while. We might as well make the effort."

"You are not going to be here for a while. But thank you for making the effort."

"You *can't* leave, and we *won't*. He's coming for you, can't you get that through your head?"

"I am not going to curl up and wilt while you do whatever it is you think you're doing to save the world."

"Damn it! What don't you see?!"

Reese's voice drawled through the open window, "Y'all don't make me come in there."

Adam's voice dropped to a hiss. "Did McConnell not just tell you what happened to his little sister?"

"So you have to take that out on everybody else? I'm sorry about Reese's sister, and the Diner Ladies, and everything! But Vertigo is a psychopath."

"Sociopath," corrected Adam.

"What. Ever." Karina could have smacked him for bringing out the 13-year-old in her. "And you? You're in it for the what, the glory? The, the wolf ears, is that it?"

"We're through here."

"Good. I'll help you get packed, or I'll go myself."

"Reese! Don't let the lady leave."

"A' right!"

Karina declared that she needed a shower and Adam retreated to the task of frying eggs and bacon, sulking.

It was going to be a long month, he realized.

Fish and House Guests

"A month!!" By the end of the day, Karina had insisted that she needed to sit out on the porch for some fresh air, at least, as the rain had cleared. She eyed the setting sun.

"We're sticking around for your safety, Ma'am," Reese's genuine concern was evident. Adam Hunter must have some slick brainwashing skills in this organization indeed. "Ma'am, Vertigo is after you and we are the only ones who can look out for you."

"This is my house! You can't stay and you can't keep me here. I've got a business to run! I have two commission meetings coming up next week."

"Well ..." Reese was nonplussed. "I mean, the whole team's looking out for you and your business. And this here is all Silverized, ain't it. All of it is. Even the trees, now. Heck, Ma'am, nothing can get in here."

"Well, Reese. Thank you. You've been very kind."

Karina allowed the front door to slam as she returned to her room, and in short order had restocked her bag. She would put some distance between herself and her house, then call the state police and let them know her property had been taken over by a bunch of nut cases looking for Bigfoot.

"There are bears out there," drawled Adam from the bedroom doorway where he'd silently been leaning. "If you aren't worried about Vertigo or desRosiers, you might consider the temper of an angry mama with her cubs. Moon or no moon." He stepped into the room and took it all in.

Karina dropped her bag onto the bed. "But using me as bait for your Junior Rangers Brigade is just fine, though? I see. Thanks, cowboy."

Adam stood aside as Karina pushed past him to get into her closet. "Reese says you're worried about your commissions next week."

"What are you planning to do about that, Tex? Drive me to Duluth?"

"I will, actually. I wouldn't let you near a bicycle right now."

Karina halted. "You will?"

"I will. Personally. Because I loooooooove your work."

"But you're still making me bait. You figure Vertigo will find me no matter where I go, right? And that Simon will come back for me. Hah, especially with the news story. How do you live with yourself? Does the mirror help? Or is it the fan mail?"

Adam did not take his cold eyes off hers.

He reached into his shirt pocket and drew out a photograph, holding it up to her. The image was dated 12 years ago.

In it, a young auburn-haired woman smiled, holding an absolutely adorable small boy whose eyes were remarkably like Adam's. They were standing next to a tent that had been pitched on a lawn outside a Texas-style ranch house.

"Take a good look."

A terrible chill crept through Karina's toes and seeped into her bone marrow. "Your family …"

"They were killed that same night. Adam Jr. wanted to play camping, so Mary Beth made up a little campsite in the yard." He couldn't go on.

"Vertigo?"

Adam's jaw worked as he ushered her into the living room to sit on the sofa. He retrieved a manila envelope from a file on the bookcase and held it up. He'd composed himself some-what, and spoke softly. "This is my last resort with you."

Moving next to her, he pulled out a series of photos and tossed them onto the coffee table. Karina didn't know what she was looking at. Then objects took shape—a hand here, a shredded leg—she pushed them away, sickened.

Adam shoved them back harshly. "Take a good look. You think that night when Deputy Moore was killed was rough? Look at it! Those were your Diner Ladies. That—" he jabbed the photos that Karina couldn't look at, "is what you are refusing to see! That," he spat, "is what I found when I ran outside, when the screaming started, when the howls began, and I found my …" he was shaking violently. "My wife, and my baby."

Karina would have stood up if she'd been able.

"Vertigo—"

"It doesn't matter, woman! Vertigo, desRosiers, they're all the same. Can't you get that into your skull? They're all the same!" He leaned into her, holding up the photo of his wife and child, hissing, "But for my family, it was desRosiers."

PIT OF FIREWOLVES

Vertigo in his human form rolled around in the mud and dead leaves north of Karina's guest house, deep in the woods.

His shrieks of laughter rousted birds from the trees and stilled all other sounds. This was going to be another easy one! And his own reinforcements were coming on all sides for the next moon. But tonight, tonight belonged to him alone. Hunter, that ridiculous boy who'd sniveled for days over his pretty little wife and child, was coming right to him, bringing that tender morsel of a girl with him for a little thrilling personal time. And desRosiers would be certain to follow, his anger blurring all reason.

Silly child, that Simon. He'd had a bad habit of interfering with Firewolf attacks, but he hadn't been able to stop that one way back in Texas. Ah, he reminisced, such fun he'd had! The chaos! And with the black wolf desRosiers being the only one spotted that night, Vertigo had gotten clean away with it. That sniveling boy Adam Hunter would never be able to keep up with the truth. Interesting twist, that Silverizing thing, though.

Vertigo would get desRosiers soon, and then he'd likely be

able to stop his own infernal policing of the Firewolf pack. With a little more luck, he'd even get his little toy Jake back.

But for now, he'd commandeered the ground around the Hunters' headquarters. He'd known about the place for moons now, and waited patiently until the Hunters began to make their way north from Texas to pursue a desRosiers sighting.

Vertigo knew that Adam had called in all available members of the Hunter pack, as he must have suspected that there would soon be a gathering of wolves up here in the woods. Once Hunter and a couple of other gray playthings had arrived at the Redfeather house, all Vertigo had to do was cause some trouble to keep them in place, and then wait for the games to begin. Come this night, there would be no more Adam Hunter, desRosiers would be finished, he'd have Jake back in his thrall, and he could keep the girl for fun.

By next moon, all the remaining wolf lines would be here, along with the full complement of Hunters avenging their leader. Or, wait, wouldn't it be even more fun to turn Adam Hunter and set his own men after him? The joys were endless. So many possibilities, and all started by a vengeful Hunter seeking his family's killer and dragging his whole pack after him. He really ought to slow down and think this through.

Vertigo's own pack would be waiting for their leader, right in his own headquarters. He howled and shrieked into the treetops and covered himself in leaves again, rolling and laughing. In stalking desRosiers, the Hunters were, of course, chasing the wrong wolf, and bringing the whole party straight to Vertigo himself.

Creek Run Update: Artist Karina Redfeather Revealed to be in Protective Custody

Pigeon Creek—Members of the self-proclaimed Hunters based at the home of Pigeon Creek resident Karina Redfeather have issued a statement saying that the artist is under protection at her home in Pigeon Creek.

"Miss Redfeather is not considered an accomplice in the recent murders at Pigeon Creek, and has been placed under our protection for her own security. She will remain here safely until this situation can be resolved," noted Adam Hunter in a statement emailed to the *Creek Run* late last night.

The *Creek Run* attempted to contact Hunter, but neither he nor anyone else related to the organization was available, and phone messages were not returned.

During a phone call made to the Minnesota state police, Lt. Brock Sherman explained that no complaints had been received by anyone in the area. Because Miss Redfeather is not actually missing and has filed no reports, there is no reason to become involved. When asked about the possibility of werewolves in the area, Lt. Sherman abruptly terminated the call.

No further information is available at this time.

UPDATED: In the absence of a sheriff, Adam Hunter was elected to office last night by the remaining seven residents of Pigeon Creek by a margin of six to one.

###

Hunters and Gatherers

In the next few days, the Hunters stationed outside kept mostly to themselves, their vans and campers providing them with whatever they seemed to require. Every so often one of them would pause by the largest tree, head bowed; from time to time, they would stoop to place something on the growing little heap below the heavy branches. It dawned on Karina what had become of Bill's badge. In spite of the horror of it all, she had a fit of irrepressible giggles at the thought of the way Simon's wolf would happily treat that spot under the tree.

The Hunters operated in teams of two, and Karina caught sight of an older and younger woman who might easily have been mother and daughter. The groups' accents were from several regions around the country. All of the Hunters seemed focused and professional, giving Karina no cause for complaint aside from their continued existence. Meanwhile, Adam had left a printout of the Creek Run's latest dispatch lying conspicuously on the coffee table.

There was little talk in the cottage over the next few days, and even less sleep. Reese was the only one with an appetite.

Horrible dreams haunted Karina in the few tossing, turning hours that she did get. Reese turned Firewolf and dragged
her through the woods. Simon chased her relentlessly in both
human and wolf form. A sweet little boy was torn to shreds
before her, and she woke up hoarse and wet-eyed.

There was so much Simon had never told her. She tried to
imagine what his lover might be like, and whether she was a
Waterwolf, as he was. Or maybe there was a fourth bloodline
after all, and he was nobly assisting them as well? How long
might they have known one another? There would be so much
he did not have to explain to this woman. That part made
sense, yet she could not stop torturing herself over it.

But these murder accusations of Adam's didn't add up.
Hadn't Simon protected her, and told her that the thrill was in
the chase, and that he would avoid a house, like any wild
thing? *Like any wild thing* ... But being near a ranch house,
with the scent of livestock around, and people outside in a
tent; could it have been tempting? Maybe it had been Apex,
and perhaps something had irritated the wolf in him?

What was she thinking? Adam was right, she was making
excuses for Simon, in spite of everything she now knew. Well,
then; was Adam right? Really?

Sharing her own space with two men she wasn't overly
fond of was beginning to wear, too. They were all doing their
best, but the situation was awkward, and the few days it had
lasted had dragged on by the minute. Still, aside from Reese,
Adam would not permit any of the other Hunters—not even

the mother-daughter team she'd strongly requested—to remain in the house for long. They'd been an interesting pair, those two, and she'd have liked a break to chat longer than ten minutes with them.

And now? Now Adam Hunter had the added authority of having been elected Sheriff. Insufferable.

Reese was just as sweet as ever, and Karina felt nibbles of remorse for him, as he tried to make some sort of peace between her and Adam. She'd heard him speak his mind about Adam's ruthless display of the crime scene photos, but Adam was unrelenting in his stance that it had been the only way to make her see sense.

And there wasn't much to say; all Karina had now were questions. If anyone could tell her something of the Fourth Bloodline, it would be one of the Hunters, but she dared not ask.

For now, she'd extracted from Adam the promise of transportation to the city so she could settle her two small contracts; and in return, she'd given her word to accept the situation she was in.

She was utterly, completely defeated.

Through all this time, there were rumors across the woods of the Firewolves' northward advance, and of a convening of the Bloodlines at the next moon.

Hearing of this, the elusive band of the Fourth Bloodline was roused and on the move, steadily making its way through the territory surrounding Pigeon Creek.

New Moon

"Music and beer," declared Greg in the moody and silent late afternoon, so Tyler and Simon followed along and found their way into a dive bar tucked down the side street of a borderline ghost town far off the beaten track. The place was barely more comfortable indoors than out, dank and chilly, reeking of the stale beer that stuck to the soles of their boots and crackled with each step on the filthy linoleum floor.

A slack-jawed, sleepy-voiced young singer strummed a lament about her ex-boyfriend not being in touch with her true self, as an equally slack-jawed and sleepy clientele nursed their bottles. One of them moved dizzily toward the bare patch of wooden floor that delineated it as a tiny stage, beer in hand, and tried to sing along, his lack of consonants matching his dance skills.

"I'd kill for a juke box," pronounced Greg.

"A what?" Tyler looked up from his burner cell phone.

Greg shot him a lethal glance. "Have you ever even seen a book?"

Simon's eye fell on a chipped, gluey bar table by the greasy window, with a view of the bleakness outside. He settled at one of the tall stools while his companions tried to wrangle anything but a watery beer from the bar's limited offerings.

Simon's attention drifted back outside, where a feral cat huddled near some soggy cardboard boxes, warily eyeing up passersby. The sight of the shaking creature drew him deep into dark memories of a time long in his past, back when it had all begun and he strolled shadowed streets, avoiding even the anonymous, sultry calls from darkened recesses.

He'd seen that same wide-eyed, haunted look on a soul-beaten girl, a new one, shivering and stamping her sandaled feet in a doorway. He'd doubled back to a takeout window to get her some hot coffee and a sandwich, but she wouldn't take it, nor would she accept his offer of help. Defeated, and knowing they were both being watched by her owner, Simon retreated. A shuddering addict in the next alleyway got the lukewarm meal instead. It seemed that the whole world trembled in the cold pain of a living death.

Greg knocked him back into to the present with a cloudy glass of what smelled like cheap whisky and old memories. The cat was gone, and the sleepy-voiced singer moved offstage, watching everything intently. Inhaling deeply, she carried her guitar out the side door. Her groggy suitor staggered after her, sobering up awfully fast as she turned from the new-moon evening and stared at him with eyes ringed in the palest blue.

First Date

Karina moved gracefully down the porch steps and almost defiantly, faced the car where Adam stood transfixed. Gone were the paint-splattered jeans and Simon's baggy flannel shirts. Her hair was up in an Audrey Hepburn sweep, and the long brown leather coat over her gold knit dress matched her simple heels and portfolio. Adam lost all power of speech.

She allowed him to hold the car door for her, but her eyes could have killed him. He couldn't muster a single smart remark and guessed that she knew it.

This was the way he'd seen her photographed in art magazines, and in her brief TV press interviews as she tried, almost in vain, to usher the attention back to her work during this opening or that one.

"You wore that dress at the New York gallery opening," he blurted.

"I didn't realize that you were a collector," Karina retorted, drilling her eyes into him.

"I am, actually." The road to Duluth blurred and sped beneath them. "Well, sculpture, not paintings. But it's still art," he finished lamely.

She was silent for a moment and then relented, dancing around the edge of a civil discourse on galleries and artists that they both found they admired. The conversation lost a little of its chill over the miles, and by the time they reached the first client, at an upscale hotel in Duluth, it was almost human.

He reminded her that he'd be back to join her for dinner at the second client's restaurant. As he drove off, Adam found himself daydreaming about his days as a 6th-grade schoolboy with a crush on his teacher. His eye was caught by a menswear store and he pulled over to kill some time.

When he arrived at the restaurant to meet Karina a few hours later, there was a slight hush as he strolled in.

A dozen pairs of feminine eyes followed the tall, icy-eyed man in the blue turtleneck and black suede jacket to see whether he might, possibly, be approachable at the bar. When he reached Karina's table, the disappointment surrounding the two of them was almost audible.

Karina concentrated on her sparkling water. A couple of sideways glances at him only made him lean in closer.

"How did it go?"

"They're happy, thanks."

Their waiter ghosted by to fill their water glasses, and Karina addressed him in perfect Russian.

"So," Adam was nonplussed. "How many languages do you speak?"

"A few," Karina picked up her knife and frowned at it.

"You studied in Russia?"

"My mother was Russian."

"I thought you were Cherokee?"

"My father was Ojibwe."

"Ah."

"It's not something I talk about," Karina said softly.

A brief silence chilled their plates. Adam tried again.

"Have you eaten here before? You have?" There was the quiet click of a camera nearby.

Karina nodded. "We used to come here sometimes when I was little. My mother was friends with the original owner, but his son Petrov has taken over. They wouldn't give me a menu," Karina added, looking around from the alcove table for the waiter, with no luck.

"No, um ..." Oh, this wasn't going to go well. "I asked them to do something special for us. It's, well ... You haven't ..."

Karina leveled burning eyes on his.

"Ah, hell, I'm hungry. You ready to eat?"

"This is not a date."

"No, but it is a nice place, and I guess you're celebrating a couple of commissions, so ..."

Oh, let's just get this over with, Karina thought, and must have rolled her eyes. When Adam looked at her, he seemed almost boyishly hurt; he'd been tousling his hair nervously, and he was trying so hard. For a moment he looked almost ... likable.

"Well, I suppose it is a sort of a celebration. I guess, normally ..." she offered a white flag, "normally I just go straight home."

"Well now, that's a shame," Adam's smile was genuine, dazzling. "And I hope you don't mind champagne."

A horrible thought struck Karina's stomach. "I have to be back home tonight."

Adam grinned wickedly. "No, you don't. But on my honor as a Texan, Ma'am, I will have you home tonight, unscathed."

Karina really looked at him this time. "Maybe for now," she reminded him. "But I believe I am still monster bait."

Adam returned her gaze. "You're not, you know." The champagne arrived. "You have to eat. Might as well enjoy it. Look, I know you like Reese, but this would be totally wasted on him." Karina had to smile at that. "He'd be asking for a cheeseburger. With chili on it to make it all fay-ancy."

Karina laughed in spite of herself. "Stop it. He's a sweet guy, for a Hunter."

"Well, they can't all be like me. Here's to your eyes."

He raised his glass and Karina had to look away.

Petrov had outdone himself with the evening, and by the time dinner was over, Karina had managed to relax a little.

Just after they'd finished their coffee, a little boy with a deep drawl approached the table with a pen and a napkin.

"Ess'cuse me," he said shyly, "are you Mr. Hunter?"

And so ended the meal, as Adam obliged his little fan with a brief chat and an autograph. The boy's parents nodded and waved at them as they got up to leave.

"Sorry," Adam said with a wink as he helped Karina with her coat. "That usually doesn't happen in the city."

"Oh, he was adorable," Karina smiled despite her aversion to the situation. "Adam? Thank you."

Adam briefly rested a hand on her shoulder, and they walked out the door to an explosion of flashing cameras and cell phones.

"Sorry," Karina smiled ruefully, speaking above the clamor, "I'm afraid this sometimes does happen to me in the city!" She waved shyly, until a brute of a paparazzo pushed a younger man aside and started yelling at them about werewolves.

"That's enough, thank you," Adam was all business again, placing himself between Karina and the inquisitor, but the aggressive man stepped up and demanded to know what Adam and his group were going to do about it all.

Stepping back, Karina tripped on her own high heel, and as Adam caught her around the waist, another dozen cameras clicked. Petrov arrived quickly and ushered them back inside with a thousand apologies. "Oh, please don't worry, Petrov," Karina smiled, "these things happen."

Shortly, Adam's car was brought around to the back exit and they were on the way home. Once again, Adam's apologies were sincere, and Karina waved them off, saying no harm had been done.

But, of course, it had.

The Chimerae

The Rush was overtaking Tanis and she barely reached her favorite haunt in the deep woods before rolling into a den and clamping her jaws onto the resident bear's hind leg. It took only moments to convince the animal to leave, and she bounced around the walls of the earthen cave, desperately trying not to howl too loudly. It was so hard.

The exhilaration, though! Wait 'til Selena found out that she'd resisted the powerful temptation to create a new wolf. She'd just left him open-mouthed and stunned, crumpled in the alleyway trash where he belonged. And it would have been so easy, so easy, and to have her Seventh Hound would be so awesome, so cool, so, so cooooooool—the howl escaped her.

Giggles in wolf shape always came out as snuffles, which made her laugh even more. The woods had grown mightily still; there was almost a substance to this quiet. Tanis could hold on no longer, and leaping to the mouth of the cave, produced the wildest screaming howl she could manage, losing her footing, slipping backwards and rolling into a ball as she fell, snuffling, and trying to regain control. Oh, the joy, the freedom!

If only Selena could truly see how liberating this was. She would have to agree with Tanis's plans. A curse? Hah! Tanis could tell the world about curses. This wasn't close. Nowhere close. Nope. Noooooooooooooooooooooooooooo …

Tanis bounded away from the cave mouth, snapping at branches, scenting the air for a moment—was that? No, never mind. There were squirrels about, and she'd neglected to eat, spending too much time singing at the bar.

Stupid drunk dancing guy. What had saved him in the alley? His stupid breath and his stupid pawing at her. She could have had him. He'd have been at her feet, this Seventh of hers. Stupid guy. But she didn't want trash as her final Hound, nor to be around it for the rest of her life.

She stopped, tasting the air. Squirrels. Come on, squirrels. Stupid stepfather. She'd hidden from him like a squirrel. Stupid drunk guy. Stupid pawing guy. He'd have been her First Hound, but for two things. She didn't want him around forever, and in the initial fury of her early wolfhood, she'd slaughtered him. Her next raging howl escaped her. There'd been little satisfaction in the kill but he would never bother her again. And who, who would suspect a werewolf at New Moon? Whooooooooooo?

Ah, so much for the squirrel dinner. Now that bear; where had the bear gone? The blood trail was there, distracting in its promise. She dropped low and began to scent with purpose. The heart would be good, and the liver so juicy. Quietly, now, quietly. Wow. Talk about making tracks. The bear had long gone, and there went dinner. Wait … there was a whiff of human! Two … no, three … oh, she couldn't. One was a man, though, would he do? No … a woman and child, too. And terrified. Damn.

Tanis flexed her jaws and retreated, slowly wandering back to the cave, scenting as she moved. Heaven help anything else that crossed her path tonight.

But it did. It crossed from behind her, and locked its powerful jaws onto the skin at the back of her neck. Limp, whining like a puppy, Tanis allowed herself to be carried back into the cave by the Queen of the Chimerae.

It's On the Internet,
So It Must Be True

In an Internet cafe the following morning, Simon desRosiers burned his tongue while gulping a mug of coffee and staring at the *Creek Run*'s slightly blurry image of Adam Hunter, his arm tightly around Karina, whose face seemed hidden in his shoulder, and the photo caption "Where, Wolf?"

She's on the rebound already, was his first thought, but he let it go. It came back, panting like a puppy, nipping at his edges and growling. *But she can't be; she's smart, and she's perfectly capable of looking out for herself. She has to see Adam Hunter for what he is.*

A trick of the camera. It had to be. Simon squinted at the screen, but couldn't see her face or make out what might really be happening.

So what if she was rebounding from her crush on him. She ought to! He insisted on it. He had never led her on and never allowed her to act on her feelings. But now she was literally in the hands of Adam Hunter. And whose fault was that?

The hot, bitter coffee echoed his guilt. That other guilt. The one surrounding the vow he'd made to a cherished friend decades ago; the promise to protect the son, and then the granddaughter. Great. He'd managed that outcome beautifully, by delivering her right behind enemy lines.

The puppy growled again, in a voice strikingly like Greg's. "Well, well. That is a surprising turn," his friend leaned in for a closer look at the screen. "'Where, Wolf?'? Great. Just great."

Simon glanced up, "It's the *Creek Run*. Who reads it, or cares?" He clicked off the page and moved off the seat to give Greg his ten minutes.

Greg scanned through the national news pages and found the Pigeon Creek murders under "Odd News." He sighed. "I'm almost tired of running." He clicked the headline.

The stock PR image of the Hunters filled the screen, a half-dozen to the rear, and Adam's broad shoulders up front, with the ghost of a smile as his pale blue eyes drilled into the camera. The sidebar poked a little fun and suggested Roswell, New Mexico, might be the next hunting ground. "Well," Greg stroked a finger across the shot—on a full moon that would have been the living end of Adam Hunter—"nobody's buying into it yet, anyway." He rose and the two stepped into the chilly morning.

"Greg."

"Yeah."

"I need to stick around here for a few days. They're on the move."

"I know."

"Toward Rina's place," continued Simon. "I've got to ..."

"I know."

They walked a few paces together.

"And," Greg picked up the conversation, "this is yet another thing Karina doesn't know a thing about."

"Knock it off."

"Quit kidding yourself."

"I might need you tonight, Greg. If not, I'll see you after a few days." Simon peeled off at a trot, and disappeared into the woods on a path that only a few could follow.

"Yeah, and in what shape will that be," Greg said under his breath, catching up with Tyler and hailing Carl as he and Old Jake turned a corner with bags of groceries. They looked like the tramps they'd become in the past two weeks, all of them. A filthy dog darted out of a doorway, recognized Greg for what he was, and raised his hackles. Greg shook his head and reached the rest of the group, all of them turning down a long, empty road that branched off into the pine forest.

On his own path, Simon kept a steady pace for about four miles, following his memories deep into the woodlands in the opposite direction from his friends. The perspiration on his body had little to do with his exertion and grew stronger as he warily approached his destination. And there it was, two hundred feet through the trees and barely visible: a circular encampment of antique vardos, with cobalt crescent moons hanging on the doors and tiny windows of the distinctive wagons. The vardos' dappled teal and sky blues, deep purples and hazy grays would hide the camp from anyone not actually looking for it.

A tall, slender woman stepped from one of the wagons, pausing as she wrapped a long sheepskin coat around herself. She freed her hip-length black hair from inside it and looked through the dense growth directly at Simon. Her dark eyes held his shape as he moved. He'd forgotten just how acute her senses were, and how much more so they must have become in the passing of nearly forty-five years since their first meeting.

He approached quietly and slowly, all the same, and a slight smile ghosted her lips as she formed the name "Simon."

"Selena." He held his arms out and she grasped both his hands.

"Simon." Her eyes were bright as she drew him into the circle of the camp. A few caravan doors were open to the fresh air, revealing bright and welcoming interiors within their deeply muted outer colors. He recognized two or three design styles of their particular owners and was happy to note that they were still with the pack.

"Are you well?" They asked simultaneously, and with a bright laugh, Selena observed that Simon hadn't changed all that much in the eight years since the last time they had seen one another. "Usually there is something in the eyes ..." Selena trailed off, looking deeply into his. "But you are still holding well."

"So are you," he bit back her true name, "Selena. You haven't aged a moon. No, wait," he grinned mischievously. "You are even more graceful, perhaps."

"And you still speak like a badly written novel," she teased. "Simon, it's me. No need to be so formal."

Simon flushed slightly. Selena had always been something of a supernatural person to him, figuratively as well as literally. "I've kept one of my promises," he said quietly.

"I know. Thank you," she nodded and stepped back for a longer look. Simon noticed the cobalt crescent locket falling from its intricate golden chain, and she subconsciously swept it back inside her loose shirt. "You must know why I have brought us all back here."

"I'd hoped you had heard," Simon rested his foot on a large rock and leaned back against a fir tree.

"Sit down, Simon, please. Gwen and Sayuri will be happy to see you," Selena took a seat on the rock herself. "Most of the club is out hunting before nightfall. We're short on grocery cash this month, I'm afraid, so we're relying on our own skills."

Selena hesitated a long moment before speaking again, her voice concerned. "There are only a few of us left, you know, and I'm having trouble with one of them." She gestured to a caravan, which was chained and padlocked with what seemed to be traces of silver in the links. Six men hovered nearby, trancelike, either sitting straight-backed or standing alertly outside it. Each one wore a small cobalt crescent around his neck.

"Guards?" Simon raised an eyebrow. "Really, Selena?"

"No, my dear friend. Not guards." Selena exhaled crossly. "Count them. Six. My little troublemaker seeks a Seventh Hound to close her Artemis Circle and become a new queen all on her own."

"Oh, good lord."

"I'm afraid so." Selena stretched inside her loose coat, soaking in the weak morning sunlight.

"You can't be serious. She's collecting Hounds? That's unconscionable. How dangerous is she?"

Selena's eyebrow arched as she glanced over at the little group outside the camper. "Really, Simon. She has six already; what do you think? One more and she has raised her own hunting pack. She will be uncontrollable. She in particular will be very dangerous—on a par with Vertigo."

Simon made a weak attempt at a joke, waving toward the route he'd used to find the camp. "I guess I'd better get moving before nightfall, then, or I'll be a … what would I be? I can't say I'm keen on turning twice each month."

"Fortunately for you, there is no such thing as a two-blooded wolf. You would certainly escape the bonds of being the Seventh Hound; however, you would most likely die anyway. A better outcome, perhaps."

"I dare say I ought to round up my boys and get as far away as I can, then."

"That would be best," nodded Selena. "Be careful tonight, Simon; It is the sharpest night of the moon, and I have scouts covering a 100-mile field. You must not cross them in any way." They stood up together. "Gwen and Sayuri will be happy that you stopped by. And you remember Quinsey?"

Simon nodded with a grin, "Tell her I send her a hug; see what she says."

"She would rather tell you herself," Selena laughed. "It is lovely to see you again, my dear friend, and you have kept both your promises well."

Simon couldn't look at her. "I don't think so," he mumbled. "Your son ..."

Selena's face became somber. "You did the best you could. I could neither recognize his car nor stop myself. My own son! Twice," she continued bitterly, "twice I lost him. The second time by my own doing." Simon found a patch of moss to examine for a few moments, until he heard Selena's breathing return to normal. *Not your own*, he wanted to say to her. *It was the wolf's doing.* "As for your second promise," continued Selena, "what can you tell me?"

Simon told her everything.

Her eyes grew even darker. "You left her alone? With those ... Hunter-creatures? And with Vertigo in the area? Simon!"

"Selena, it was the only option."

In the late morning rays, Selena stood, shadow of the wolf encroaching with her rising determination, and called her circle together.

"What about Tanis?" asked one of the women.

"Let her join us," responded the queen. "Simon, find Gregory right away. You and he will ride with us before it gets any later. We will all be leaving together."

"How? I mean … Selena, you could kill us later if we're even close to you."

Two women strode into camp, armed with bows and arrows and carrying freshly killed rabbits. The taller, a black woman who looked to be in her early forties, slowly took aim at him. "Hello, Simon," she grinned at him.

"Quinsey! Always a pleasure," he laughed.

"Ah, good; Quinsey, you're here. Gwen, would you tell the rest of the team to get the bikes? We are leaving within the hour, and taking Simon with us." She smiled fondly at Simon, "They are of a fellow pack, and we'll pick them up along the way."

"Sure," Gwen, a pixie-ish young woman with an easy smile, brushed her tousled blonde bob out of her eyes and looked at Simon dubiously. "This fellow pack—are they some of us?"

"Not of the crescent, but yes, they are old friends. We must leave very soon, so that we reach Pigeon Creek well before sunset."

Gwen and Quinsey rounded up their fellows, each of whom appeared with a hardy-looking motorbike that was to be loaded up with spare clothing, trail food, and the requisite coffee. Tanis was released after all the preparations had been made, spouting language that would make a sailor blush while her Hounds eyed Simon suspiciously. There was also an unsettling gleam in the young woman's eyes as they ran over Simon from head to toe and back again.

Selena gave the order and a dozen engines revved and roared. Tonight, under the sharpest crescent of the new moon, the Chimerae would hunt.

Tell Me True

Karina had been half-expecting it. The men's stares had been deeper, the voices more clipped in the past two days. Finally, the Hunters cornered her in the bright little kitchen and an FBI agent revealed himself.

"How could you!" Karina demanded. "How could *you*?!" But they clamped down on her and shackled her to a kitchen chair. She strained against the handcuffs until her wrists chafed and bled.

The interrogation wore Karina out in twelve different places. "Where is your grandmother now?" The FBI agent's badge reflected off the sunlight pouring through the kitchen window as he leaned over to adjust the voice recorder.

"She died when I was young—I told you that."

"How is Simon related to you?" Adam bent and spoke very softly from behind her, just over her shoulder.

"Put your wolf ears on, maybe they'll help!" Karina spat at him. "He's my mother's sister's son!"

"Your mother was an only child. We know a lot more than you think, Miss Redfeather. Just talk to us."

"How does Simon know your grandmother?" persisted the

Badge.

They were into their second hour of the same questions.

"Why did your grandmother stop talking to your father? When?"

"I told you. After he came back from boarding school he wasn't the same. There was a rift."

"What kind of rift?"

"He wasn't Ojibwe any more—that's what my uncle told me. It was all stolen from him at the Catlinite school. It broke her heart. They didn't speak for a long time, and she finally died."

"How?"

"I told you, I don't know! She just died! I was little. I don't know."

"And your parents?" The Badge idly flipped through a file.

"You already know. It's all in those papers! Or you can just ask Adam here, since he knows so much."

"Let's see ... eight years ago; car crash for your Dad, cancer for your Mom? What, six months apart?" drawled The Badge.

Karina's furious tears dripped onto her shirt—Simon's shirt—and she remained silent.

"Sure it was a crash? New moon, no light ... sure it wasn't something else?" Adam whispered again.

Karina sobbed an unintelligible response.

"All right. That'll do." Standing up to tuck both the digital recorder and his FBI badge back into his shirt, Reese McConnell unhooked her from the cuffs and the lie detector and left her shivering at the table.

Karina stumbled to the bedroom; carrying nothing, she slipped out the window into the cold late afternoon light and abandoned her former life.

In an instant, on her trail were a pack of Hunters, along with a raving maniac in human form—and a full contingent of Something Else.

KARINA'S TURN

"**N**ice work, Hunter," McConnell smiled as he inspected Karina's deep, muddy tracks, which led into the woods north of the property. "She's not even trying. She'll lead us right to him."

"I want desRosiers, and I don't want her hurt," Adam's jaw was squared again. "Look. She might not even know where he is."

"Oh, come on now. She'll take us right to him." The FBI agent stood and stretched. "With any luck we might get Vertigo, too, what do you think? He's got her scent. We follow her, we get all three of them."

"She's not … bait."

"Well, hell yes, she is. You ain't going soft on us, are you?" Reese chuckled and moved off into the woods with a troop of half a dozen Hunters. "You forgetting about your wife and boy, Hunter?" Reese tossed over his shoulder, laughing with the exhilaration of the hunt.

With a snarl, Adam shouldered his rifle and took off after him.

Not far from the cottage, Vertigo's ears picked up the snap

of a twig; and he caught a whiff of the woman's sweat and just a touch of fresh blood. His mark would not heal so easily, either, he grinned to himself. Almost sundown, and he was cursed at the wrong time of the month. Well, he could still have some fun. He reached into his memory to replay some of his finest, most horrific memories. His blood pulsed faster.

And so he tracked her, working himself up with every step. There was someone else nearby, too, but something wasn't right. He couldn't be bothered analyzing it as he closed in on his prey, focusing on the blood and sweat and the hint of Simon's scent from the shirt she must be wearing.

Karina headed through the undergrowth, half blinded by tears and rage. Where was Simon? How could he have abandoned her? Adam was right then, after all. But Adam was a monster—and Reese—

Karina ran smack into something that took the wind out of her; she doubled up, gasping. Whatever it was had hit her right in the midsection.

"I'm sorry," came a soft voice, grandmotherly almost. "I try not to let that happen, but I'm not very tall and people tend to run into me." A gentle hand took hers, and there was the faintest trace of hair on the palm. Karina, still bent over, looked up and into the concerned eyes of a small Japanese woman with gray-streaked hair, long baggy sweats, and just the faintest hint of a blue ring around each iris. How could this be happening?

"Come," the woman indicated a hollow log. "You must

enter here." Her voice was lightly accented, and she began to speak more urgently. "Please. You must hurry. Sunset is near." The woman's eyes were taking on a familiar luminescence and as she held out her other hand, which was heavily gloved, Karina saw chains of silver draped in it. "I will cover you up when you are inside. Listen to me. Another Chimera—like me—is coming. Do not come out. I will go away now and leave you alone." The woman shuddered and Karina lost no time in questioning her, diving inside the musty hideout to see the chains drop across the entrance, and hear them draped across the log. Then footsteps rushed away into the brush.

There was stillness for a moment, before the early darkness erupted in a nerve-shattering shriek which dissolved into a liquid howl.

Vertigo was brought up short.

It couldn't be.

He checked the moon. Its sharp crescent peeked from behind the clouds.

Another long howl, very, very near ...

They were here?

That split second nearly cost him his existence, as a force hurled itself toward him from the woods. He couldn't scent it! It was brisk mountain air, it was a fresh wind, it was ... *Where was it?*

Vertigo was struck with something he had rarely felt in nearly three hundred years, when the Firewolves attacked the caravan of Papal emissaries trudging across the plains of Tejas in New Spain. The simple wooden cross on the breast of his tunic hadn't helped him that full moonlit night. In a guilty flash he had understood, when the yellow beast slavered before him, that his old sins, those unspeakable accusations which had led to his banishment from Sevilla, had claimed their just repentance.

Not half a mile away, Adam and Reese froze.

"She's a …" Reese began.

"Not possible," whispered Adam. "I've been here at new moon. There must be—"

A number of hollow, melodious howls took up the cry.

"There must be a dozen of them," he finished quietly.

Reese hissed, "Got any silver? Locked and loaded? Good. Hell, you may need to toss your patch at 'em. Whaddaya know—what a coup, huh? They really do exist!"

Adam took off ahead of his own pack, Reese hard on his heels, a pair of gray arrows targeting the mournful cries.

Selena rose high on her toes, growling a warning to her Chimerae as her world came into focus again. Vertigo, she scented. Hunters, too. And was that Karina—oh, my; how long had it been! A stillness in the sounds told her that one of her own had her prey cornered. But there would be no other blood spilled tonight, just the one, that of the yellow dog; even though it was the sharpest of the crescent moons. Selena moved her fellows silently toward the place where Vertigo was trapped.

He was crouched low, there under a tree, near a log covered with the burning silver—how it stung Selena's eyes—but she forced herself to focus on this human beast. This creature who had found a place as a priest at the Catlinite School, where the white people had taken her son away. This monster who had effectively killed her child before he was nine years old, long before his life had finally been taken.

Selena stifled a howl and the driving need to disembowel this animal with a single claw strike, but to do so slowly, so that he would know who she was and why this was happening. Vertigo was the one, the taker of souls. The Chimera pack circled Vertigo, but held themselves back as the raggedy human beast began to howl himself and Selena crouched for the kill.

As she lunged at her foul target, a shot rang out and a silver bullet splattered low against a nearby tree trunk. The drops immolated two of her Chimerae.

The pack turned as one, each seeking a gray-shirted target. Adam Hunter reloaded, scanning his rifle sights in the direction of the sounds he was approaching. What was that—silver chains draped across that hollow log? Was Karina hidden in there? Had she known about all this?

Damn, why weren't they visible? Adam saw a flash of eyes that also caught Reese's attention and McConnell fired, missing his shot. His life ended in a flash as the Chimera wolf tore out his throat.

Tanis thrilled at the taste of fresh blood from the red-headed man. The others were occupied and she had her pick of the Hunters who had scattered and were running for their lives. She had dreamed of the crunching of bone, she had enjoyed imagining the choking sounds of clean kills; but so far, these were only the sounds of humans fleeing through the woods, gasping for breath. Under Selena, the Chimerae were not allowed to add to their number, and Tanis growled in dark disappointment.

She wheeled, and look there! Her Seventh stood before her.

What a gorgeous thing he was! Black hair, such blue, blue eyes! Mmmm, and scratches from the bushes dripped sweet-scented blood on his cheek. An excellent Seventh Hound to complete her own pack and start fresh, away from these weaklings who shied from bestowing the thrall bite. Selena would see what havoc Tanis could wreak now, and rightfully so! The world was hers, and not even Selena would be able to govern her.

Tanis crouched and approached as the Hunter fumbled for another bullet. Slowly she advanced; slowly, slowly ... it wouldn't do to have him either immolate or turn on her when she bit. She needed only to move behind him, at just the right angle.

What she didn't hear, in her highly focused quest, was the footstep just behind her as Karina slipped out of her hiding place with a silver chain in hand. Adam slid his bullet into place and raised his gun, then saw Karina fling her weapon at Tanis's wolflike form.

She missed.

Tanis lunged at Adam. Karina was at her heels, inching toward the fallen chain for another try. Tanis, sensing the silver weapon, wheeled on Karina and then squirmed aside like a bolt of lightning.

Adam, loaded and ready, nodded at Karina. She'd bought him time. The Chimera wolf weighed her options as Karina bent toward the chain and Adam aimed at the shadowy form before him.

But Tanis was fast, very fast. She whirled from Karina to try and place her bite onto the back of Adam's neck, and Karina's bloodied wrist took a dose of wolf spit.

Oh, how she screamed, wild with the poisoned sting of the curse, twisting with the convulsions of the transformation. Karina lashed and spat, her shoulder blades tingling with energy and her heart racing with the rage of what was happening.

She saw that Adam's gun was aimed at both her and Tanis, his eyes huge, and she felt an odd scorching of the air near the fallen silver chain. But that was nothing, nothing, as she lunged and tore the throat out of her bitewolf, howling into the night, her new fangs dripping blood.

Tanis's dying bulk fell upon the chain and immolated, leaving Karina unscathed.

Selena heard the querulous howl of a new wolf, and set off toward its source, breaking off pursuit of a mother and daughter Hunter team to race to the aid of the newest Chimera.

Karina turned on Adam. The shock of her new state was still horrific, but her mind was now oddly clear and overflowing with memories of the brutal treatment that Adam and Reese had put her through. They locked eyes, Hunter and wolf, in a mutual death stare, inches from one another.

Adam, shaking, watched her as she seemed to reason through the situation and to reach a decision. The cobalt-blue wolf backed away gingerly, avoiding the burning air surrounding the traces of silver, and other instincts began to take over. Turning for one last glance at the Hunter, Karina loped off into the woods to locate her new pack. The night's animal sounds, both supernatural and expected, were gone; everything seemed to hold its breath and listen.

Adam slumped to his knees, his hand brushing the wet leaves where Karina's Chimera form had slavered. He wiped the blood off the scratch on his cheek. And he realized that too late.

In that instant, he'd cursed himself.

SECRETS IN THE SUN

Karina awoke groggily, feeling slightly nauseated. She was lying outside under pine trees somewhere, suffocated by volumes of loose, soft clothing. People were there. Birds screeched in the branches above. Someone passed a moist, warm towel across her forehead and she fiercely swatted it away.

"Have you seen the sun?" a female voice asked gently.

Startled, Karina rolled to one side for a better look at the speaker. Ugh, her head hurt. Those damn birds, too. Who was this woman?

"Don't look at me, Karina. Look up; up, and face the sun," the woman continued. Such a familiar voice. Karina squinted at her and tried to push the constricting clothing away. The woman looked like someone she ought to know.

"Look up, Karina."

"Can't," she responded hoarsely.

"Karina!"

Karina shot upright. Everything was in focus now but she felt as if she had a terrible cold, weak and achy. Several women stood nearby, looking quietly concerned. The birdsong was clear and gentle now, the fleecy sweatclothes cozy and comforting. The woman kneeling in front of her cupped Karina's face in her hands and held it upwards. The sun's rays felt like warm water, cleansing and pure. Her breathing relaxed and deepened. She was able to open her eyes a little.

"So thirsty," she whispered.

"Not right at the sun, darling, just look up."

Presently Karina felt almost normal, and the woman handed her a cup of water. She saw the others withdraw. There was something familiar…

Karina swallowed and turned to thank the woman, jarring to a stop.

"Good morning, Karina," Selena's eyes were full of emotion.

Without another word, Karina threw herself into her grandmother's arms.

Simon, on the other hand, was inconsolable. His early morning pacing had given way to a numbed silence. He sat on a rock in a close grove of pine trees, about a thousand yards from the Chimerae's temporary morning camp, Greg leaning beside him.

Sayuri, the woman who had aided Karina the night before, had paused to see if Simon had any immediate questions, but disappeared after quietly bringing the men blankets, some beef jerky, and coffee just after sunrise. All of it remained untouched.

"They don't bite like that," Simon had kept repeating the night before. "The Chimerae don't want to spread the curse."

He and Greg had been following the Hunters into the woods in an attempt to protect Selena when they came upon the attack.

"Some do; and we know that Tanis actively wanted to," Greg had responded, "and that had nothing at all to do with you." But Simon could not be calmed.

Images of Karina's attempts to save Adam played over and over before his eyes. Tanis, the Chimera wolf, had been fixed on Adam Hunter, waiting for an opportunity to seize him and render him as her final Hound.

Greg read his thoughts. "Simon, there was nothing you could do. If you'd called out to Karina, Tanis might have killed the both of you. Then Adam would have been her Seventh Hound anyway, and she'd have had her killer pack."

It was weak consolation, and Greg knew it. There was nothing else he could think of to say. Without speaking of it, he and Simon shared a feeling of guilt and weakness about having to run for their own safety and abandon Karina to her new fate.

"Imagine how she'd have felt if she'd killed you," Greg offered yet again. "And there was at least one other Chimera right about where we were. We had to leave. Come on, Simon, give yourself a break."

Suddenly Simon stood up, as Selena and her granddaughter approached, Gwen not far behind. Karina now wore baggy black leggings and a gold chain with a cobalt crescent over a clean blue sweatshirt that hung loosely around her.

Greg's impulse to talk a fresh wolf through the new experiences was powerful, particularly in light of a first kill. Never mind the circumstances, that one was always a tough thing to handle. Still, he moved away from the three as they approached one another, allowing Selena to do her job as pack leader. Seeing this, Gwen invited him to walk back to a breakfast campfire where the other Chimerae were seated.

There were only a few of them present; two of the men—Tanis's "Hounds"—had been immolated the previous night. Greg was surprised to find an air of relief among the surviving Chimerae.

"It is sad, to a certain degree. But we do not approve of collecting an Artemis Pack," Sayuri said firmly.

"We look after one another," explained Gwen. "Tanis was not the kind of person we need in our pack. I guess it is sort of sad, but she was bad news. Now we don't have to worry about her any more, and now we have Karina! Oh, sorry ..." Gwen noted the dark look fall across Greg's countenance. "I mean, we're all we have. We will look out for her, I promise!" She smiled brilliantly and seated Greg across from her, handing him a mug of coffee from a giant pot. "We take extra care of the new people. We even try and make it fun!"

Greg shook his head. "Fun? Well, I'd like some help with that." His attempt to chuckle lacked any mirth, and he changed the subject. "In all my years, I have never heard about an 'Artemis Pack.' What the heck *is* that?"

The remaining four men who'd been camped outside the imprisoned Tanis's caravan laughed wryly as Sayuri explained. "If one of the Chimerae—we are usually women—wants to start her own hunting pack, she enslaves seven men as her Hounds of Artemis. She does this with a bite that grips, at the back of the neck, not just one that inflicts the curse. This passes an extra dimension to the curse. You will see, now that Tanis is gone, that the men are no longer in thrall."

The men nodded.

"You mean the curse is broken?" Greg's coffee mug paused inches from his lips. If Vertigo died, perhaps the curse of madness on Old Jake could be lifted?

"No, sadly, no. Only the thrall is lifted. As you see, your friend Karina is now one of us in spite of the death of Tanis."

"But ... I'm thinking that one of us, well ... he was bitten as a little boy by a Firewolf. He's not like the rest of us. We thought it was because his bitewolf tortured him for decades, until our pack got hold of him. But maybe it was a, what kind of bite do you call it?" Greg leaned forward, "I mean, maybe if we can destroy the bitewolf himself, we can destroy the madness."

Sayuri shook her head. "I am sorry to say that in your friend's case I do not know. But this Firewolf; he must be the one they call 'Vertigo.' He is well known for inflicting this kind of thrall bite."

"If Jake could be ... normal," Greg trailed off.

Sayuri reached over to pat his hand. "I understand your hope," she smiled, "but in this situation, it is unlikely. We have all heard of Jake; it is a heartbreaking case. His madness is probably from the abuse. Of course, I cannot say for certain."

"Worth a try, though. I mean, we want to get Vertigo anyway, but hey, that would be a bonus. Damn," he shook his head. "Worth a try," he repeated softly as Simon, Karina, and Selena approached the breakfast fire. Karina held back, unsure of Greg's reception, but he rose to step forward and embrace her warmly.

"Gentlemen," Selena began, "we have two more cycle nights, and a new wolf to care for. Although we know you and have your scents, it would be wise for you to retreat until after that. We will ride you back to your campsite, and then, of course, you are welcome to join us back at ours when our cycle ends. You should be there when we burn the cursed caravan and purify the space."

"I'm staying right with you," declared Simon.

"You are not," replied Greg and Selena as one voice.

"Go on," Karina came to him and took his hand, noting an odd vibration in the touch. "I'm safe here," she attempted a joke, "finally." But her eyes were filling with tears. "Simon, I killed somebody."

"I know. I know." Simon took both her hands now, and spoke gently. "It wasn't really you. Selena's explained this to you, hasn't she? You know you saved all those men from the thrall curse, don't you?"

Great tears fell from Karina's cheeks as she nodded. "But that's not why I did it. I was so angry. So angry!"

"New wolves bite hardest," Simon reminded her quietly. "Just follow Selena's lead. Stick by her, and get to know your new friends here. I've known some of them for decades; they're terrific. You'll see."

"Simon. Time's moving. Come on." As Greg put an arm around Simon's shoulders, the two men thanked the Chimerae for their hospitality. The other Chimera men were approaching on their motorbikes, and motioned Greg and Simon to join them.

As Selena had already taught her, Karina breathed deeply, taking in their scent so that it would remain with her after the crescent moonrise that night.

The Help

Adam, wearing a fresh uniform with the patch ripped off, was wrapped in a blanket and drinking bourbon straight from the bottle.

The clock struck eight as the morning slowly illuminated Karina's kitchen, but no amount of looking into the sunlight would erase the nightmare he had just survived.

He replayed the immediate aftermath of Karina's turn. All he had done was lose his nerve for that one moment, that one single moment when he needed to stay alert.

She had been trying to help him. After everything he and McConnell had dragged her through just hours earlier, she was driven to help rather than destroy. And it would have been so easy for her just to stay put. If he had been in her position, after all they had put her through, he could have watched Tanis kill without blinking, never mind intervening. Perhaps it was not so black-and-white to Karina, though ... she had a quality ... could she possibly care what happened to him? It was too late to know now. The Karina he knew was gone.

And so, in fact, was he.

As daylight misted into existence through the kitchen window, Adam contemplated his Pigeon Creek Sheriff's Department badge, which still lay on the kitchen table after he'd removed it to interrogate Karina. McConnell's disappearance would be easy to explain; he had, after all, been the only FBI cryptozoology agent assigned to this area, and had been undercover at that. His report to the agency only need include his discovery of the body after the next full moon.

If he even lived that long himself.

So much for the Chimerae being a tale to scare other werewolves into submission. So much for the Hunters.

These nearly invisible Howlers had sure done a good job with his team. By ones and twos, the Hunters had timidly knocked on the door to let him know they were heading home. They hadn't signed up for this. Why hadn't he told them?

Red-eyed and unwashed, he'd waved them away. Sure, he said, it was more than he'd bargained for, too, but what did they think they were up against?

Half of them didn't even believe in the silver bullets any more. He heard some of the property being vandalized for its silver threading before the traitors burned rubber leaving the grounds.

Bastards.

He took another swig and glared bleary-eyed at three Hunters who'd just trudged in, badges intact, and before they could speak, Adam told them exactly where they could go and what they could do to themselves all the way there.

"Well, now, Boss," the tallest began, "I'm Harris, this here is Jones, and that's Vasquez. We're staying put."

"What?"

"We're with you, Boss. The Four Hunter—um, Hunter-skeers, or um Hunter-steers, or—" Harris fumbled, "Hunter-teers! That's it. All for one and Howlers for us." Adam sent him a lethal stare as he took another swig. "Hey," continued Harris, oblivious to everything but the sound of his own voice, "all the more glory for the four of us, right boys?"

Four of them. Well, three now, to fight hell-knew-what was coming, and he couldn't be a direct part of it. But a spark of an idea began to catch.

"Here," Adam passed them the bottle. "Think it over. There are still two more nights to go with this crowd before the whole mess hits in two weeks." He himself planned a night or two in the guest house. If there was any silver there, he now knew he could sense it. And if not, well, a happy ending to Adam Hunter.

"We'll get back at them, Boss, don't worry. And if not, well, we got all this silver. Odds are with us, right? And they ain't comin' in the house, that's for sure. We can shoot all those Howlers through the windows. Psshhheewww, psheeewww!!"

Outside the kitchen window, two figures crouched low, listening keenly to the news about the Hunters' reduced numbers. Gwen and Quinsey exchanged grins, delighted with the information they could take back to their little family.

"Sayuri will appreciate this," Gwen laughed as they raced back to where the others were preparing to ride out. "The number four means death in Japan."

Girl Talk

"**D**rinks before dinner!" Gwen tousled her short blonde hair, poured some champagne into a crystal glass and handed it to Karina. "Here, honey. We always carry some luxuries, even on the road!"

"We can't, surely we can't!" Karina protested, then watched her grandmother, chatting with Sayuri over by her wagon, take a sip of hers. "But ... isn't that dangerous? I mean, won't we really go crazy with this?"

Quinsey joined them on some cushions spread out below the steps of Gwen's caravan, with its doors swung wide open to display the bright pastels of its interiors. Gwen favored a Santa Fe Bohemian style, with long fabrics draped among the pillows, and the remains of incense smoking lightly on a plate by the stove. A small cooking fire was all they needed to prepare the night's meal.

"Oh, no," Quinsey held out her glass to be filled. "It wears off right at the change. Seriously! Don't worry about it. Besides, what else are we going to have with this faaaaaaaabulous fish?" She flipped the freshly caught trout in the pan over the fire. "Eat up; that's the dangerous part. Not eating."

"I ..." Karina began.

Selena had now joined the little group by the fire. "Karina, it's all right. Really. It's not like having an empty stomach; it wears off as soon as the change occurs. Just enjoy yourself. We do this sometimes at Crescent. Not always, of course, but this is a special occasion."

"Get as tipsy as you want!" giggled Gwen. "Watch!" and she downed her glass in a single gulp.

"Gwen, really—no need to make an extravagant point," admonished Selena, but Quinsey had followed suit and was already popping a second cork.

Karina joined in the laughter as the bubbles went up her nose, "Imagine if people knew about this—everybody would want to become a Chimera!"

Quinsey leaned over, clutching her tipping flute, "Karina ... or maybe they would want to become any kind of werewolf. Either that or more likely, everyone would claim to be a teetotaler so they wouldn't be suspected. What do you think started Prohibition?" and the whole party started laughing.

"Won't the men feel left out over there?" asked Karina.

"Not at all," Quinsey reassured her. "They get enough girl talk as it is. I think they have whisky tonight, anyway, don't they? Didn't Ray bag a deer?" She leaned back into the deep cushions beside the caravan. "I don't know why whisky goes with deer, but I guess whatever makes you happy." She raised her glass to the flames. "Drink up, ladies!"

"Ah, Prohibition," mused Gwen, raising her glass in return. "That was … interesting."

"You were there? You actually lived through that?" Karina turned from the warm fire to place her full attention on Gwen.

"Oh, I did indeed. Here, honey, keep your moon clothes nearby or change now, whatever's easier." Gwen tossed Karina a small pile of clothes consisting of a billowy shirt and wide pants tied loosely at the ankles. "At some point, like when we're not safe in camp, you'll want to try going *au naturel*, the way we usually do, so we can't be seen at all. You know, the Fullmooners try to keep their pants on, but that only works sometimes." That sent both Gwen and Quinsey further into laughter. Gwen caught her breath long enough to add, "I suspect you are something of the modest type, though, am I wrong?"

Karina, grateful for not having to explain herself, moved off toward the trees. "Thank you. I'll be right back."

"No bras!" Gwen and Quinsey shouted in unison, and Karina had to smile as she slipped behind a stand of pines to change. She'd never had sisters or close women friends, and was utterly unused to female companionship. In spite of everything, this could almost be fun.

Selena had retreated by the time Karina reappeared and Gwen refilled her glass. "Supper's ready—there you go. Eat up, 'cause if you don't you might go after something else. Chipmunks come back up on me," Gwen turned to Quinsey. "Do they do that to you?"

Quinsey stretched out, "No, I go for rabbits. Only if I have to! Don't be stingy, girl, hand over some of that fish!" Her ebony arm glowed against the flames in the waning afternoon. She was wearing a loose, deep blue track suit that somehow looked stunning on her. Catching Karina's eye, she laughed. "You know, Gwen's right. If you really want to blend in, you'll want to go completely natural. It's actually safer that way." With a wink, she added, "Okay, maybe not tonight. But heck, I'm only wearing this because we have company!"

Gwen turned on Quinsey and looked her up and down. "Ugh. You are not wearing that old thing again!"

"Why not? What do you want, a werewolf in a red bikini?" And they almost fell over laughing again. "Don't! Don't spill it, this is the good stuff!" Quinsey spluttered.

Sayuri joined them briefly, and declined the wine. "Selena and I will patrol tonight before sunset," she explained. "We will be sure that nobody is nearby." Her gray-streaked hair was tied up in a braid and she wore a loose outfit similar to Karina's.

There was still a good ninety minutes to go, but everything seemed ready. The pack appeared to be using the time to get into a good mood, teasing one another and telling stories.

"How are you doing, honey?" asked Gwen sympathetically, breaking from the hilarity.

"I think I'm okay." Karina untangled her long shirt, which had crumpled underneath her as she turned back and forth to speak with her new pack members. "How will it be tonight?

My grandmother—well, Selena—told me the first time is usually the worst, and it's not as bad after that, once you get used to it. And then, after a while, it can be kind of—"

Quinsey and Gwen snorted champagne through their giggles and waited for her to continue.

"But I still feel a little nervous." The source of her new friends' mirth dawned on her and she blushed a little, her last comment having just made things worse.

"Suuuuuure," Quinsey observed, cheekily. "Well, don't worry, girl, soon it will be the best fun in the world! Well, the second best."

Karina tried to derail the conversation. "Um, how did it happen to you … if it's okay to ask …"

"The night before Prohibition, of course!" laughed Gwen, still on the conversation's blue note. "My sweetie said, 'We do it now or we do it sober,' and I said, now!" and both she and Quinsey clinked glasses and laughed uproariously.

"Why, honey, you really are a shy one, aren't you!" Gwen relented. "Remember your first time? Wait." She sent Karina a searching look. "Haven't you ever been with … well, now, you never have! Honest?"

Karina was red as a beet by now and fervently wishing for the sun to set.

"Really!" Quinsey perked up. "But aren't you and that Fullmooner a couple?"

"No," Karina shot back. "Sorry. I mean, no. We're not."

Both women nodded sympathetically. "Oh, he's the one,

though, isn't he?" Gwen asked gently.

"No, not really."

"Uh-hunh." Quinsey leaned back into the cushions again. "Well, you have bigger things than that to worry about right now." She couldn't help herself and started laughing again.

"All right, leave the girl alone!" Gwen came to Karina's rescue with a smile. "You wanted to know how it happened. Well, most of us have good stories, all right. Mine was leaving the midnight show in Chicago—I was a dancer; I still am, you'll see!—and I was taking a back alley route. I liked to avoid the Stage Door Johnnies, you know? All those grabbers. I figured the darker the night, the safer I'd be. Easy to sneak through the back streets." She sighed. "Who knew? So, I pass this big dark dog rummaging through the trash, and then ..." she trailed off.

Quinsey picked up quietly with, "I was running. Fall of 1862, I was trying to get out of South Carolina. We traveled by the darkest nights possible. There were always spooky stories, but we thought they were trying to scare us into staying put." She stared into the fire. "I was the only survivor. I'll tell you what, though," she reached over to pick up the bottle and refill her glass, "crazy as it is, this life is still better than that one. By a thousand times."

Gwen continued with Sayuri's story. "She's newer. She was in an internment camp in Santa Fe in the early forties. She told me she wanted to see her brother, you know they separated everybody, right? She sneaked out of the women's Quonset hut one dark night, 'cause someone told her they were taking him away somewhere else and she wanted to say goodbye to him. Poor Sayuri ..." she smiled ruefully. "Her bitewolf wasn't hunting her, it was hiding from her. She didn't see it and she stepped on its tail."

"Oooooooh!" Everyone winced.

"As for me, I wanted to see my son." Selena's voice came quietly across the camp as she moved into view. "He was at the Catlinite School for Indian Re-education, where they kept all the Indigenous children. Everyone, from everywhere, from many tribes." Her voice grew low and husky, but the tone had nothing to do with the coming moonrise. "I tried to sneak in to the grounds. I saw there were young men and women, along with very little ones.

"Karina, you may not be surprised to hear that it was Simon who helped me get there, once he knew my story. He knew about this—this Vertigo animal, you see." Selena paused. "And I told Simon about my son being taken to the school to be 're-educated and assimilated.' Simon promised to help me get him back.

"He was following me, to help me if he could. It was the darkest night of the moon. I was ... stopped. Taken by the bite, there and then. Like you, I killed my bitewolf. But I let Simon be. And then I disappeared."

Karina stared at her, swatting to the back of her mind all the questions about how her grandmother and Simon had met in the first place. "I thought ... we were told that you and Dad couldn't get along because he wasn't the same anymore. Because of the school. And because he married my mother. That's what they told me."

Karina looked deep into her grandmother's eyes, and the pain in them shocked her.

"Yes," Selena blinked hard. "It's not the truth, but it is what I let everyone believe, after that. Of course, I did stay nearby. I think you remember once, when you were about five? It was the last time." She turned away, unable to continue.

A dreadful silence enveloped the group.

A man's voice called over, "Too quiet over there. Smile, sweeties!" Quinsey shouted, "Come over here and say that, Baby! I'll eat you up!" A chorus of laughs floated from the men's fireside, and the overall mood rose a little. Soon they were back to a more comfortable state as the sun lowered, and they began to separate.

Karina stayed near her guardian, as a new wolf should, and the night proceeded without incident.

The Unholy Alliance

"Don't they call that sleeping with the enemy?" Harris stretched his tall frame across two chairs in what used to be Karina's kitchen, leaving small mud cakes everywhere. Dishes were piled in the sink, and Harris was drinking sun tea from the same jar he'd been using for two weeks. The first night of the full moon was approaching at sunset of the following day, and Adam's remaining three followers were still arguing among themselves about plans to destroy the last of the Howlers.

"And your idea is what, Genius?" observed Vasquez to Harris. "Boss, I think your idea could work." *Mighty big of you,* thought Adam. "Yeah, it could. Get Vertigo and his Howlers on our side to take out desRosiers, then ambush 'em all. Yeah. I like it, Boss."

Adam, sporting a two-week beard growth, rubbed his hand across his chin but said nothing.

"Who's going in first to talk to them, then ... *Genius?*" Harris sulked back.

Jones, meanwhile, with his dark and self-important moodiness, had the unfortunate ability to remind Adam of his former associate William J. Moore; there was always one, wasn't there? Still miffed that he wasn't being officially deputized, Jones sat stiffly near the stove and contributed a very clear level of nothing.

After a prolonged silence, Adam stood up, shouldered a regular shotgun, and checked his sidearm—briefly considering using it on all four occupants of the room.

"I'll be back in an hour," he stated, striding out of the kitchen. His three companions armed themselves and hurried through the untidy living room and down the front porch steps to catch up with him. Adam pointedly ignored them.

"Vertigo!" Adam shouted several times as he approached the Firewolves' camp. "Coming in, need to talk."

"And we're armed!" added Jones.

"Here's some advice," offered Adam, quietly. "Shut up."

Filthy, rancid, and chaotic-looking, the Firewolves' camp was enough to turn anyone's stomach. Remains of animals lay in a pile under a bush, and apparently none of the pack members strayed too far away in order to relieve themselves. Strewn about were glossy magazines with images that Adam couldn't bring himself to examine. The camp seemed to be deserted.

"See, Adam?" trumpeted Jones. "Scaredy cats!" With both hands, he held his rifle triumphantly above his head and whooped.

The firearm was immediately snatched from behind him.

"Surrender, do you?" hissed Vertigo.

Adam wheeled on them both. "Drop it, Padre."

For Vertigo, the world disappeared, and had no focus except for Adam Hunter. "What did you just say?"

"You heard me."

Vertigo held the rifle out to one side and gently put it down. This was going to be a very interesting conversation indeed.

After the new moon cycle had ended, the Chimera band regrouped with Simon, Greg, and the rest of their pack at their vardo camp.

New and happier plans were afoot, and everyone knew what was left to do before they moved on. Preparations to burn Tanis's former caravan were well under way, since nobody else wanted to live in it. The former thrall men were gleeful at the thought of its destruction and the new freedom of simply camping outside.

Selena's Chimerae, knowing how to make the best of everything, had sent out a call to the approaching packs, so that this, the final night before the full moon's onset, would be one to remember.

As for the two packs eventually splitting up, the mountains were probably a good choice for Simon and his friends, Selena had told them. Far away, in Colorado. The Chimerae would consider heading back to their winter compound outside Santa Fe, instead of waiting for the cold weather as they usually did.

They would see how Karina felt, given her unexpected instability, but it would be infinitely safer than keeping her here.

This particular morning, Quinsey quietly left a large mug of coffee next to Karina, who was sitting in a tight ball beneath the roots of a tree, her head in her arms, sobbing.

As Selena returned to the campfire, she spoke with Perry, one of Tanis's four surviving former thralls, who shook his head sympathetically as he watched Karina. "I kind of feel that way myself today," he observed to Selena.

"No doubt," replied the leader. "You have suffered in your own way, under the circumstances, and you are only now coming to terms with this as well."

"Can't we do something?" Gwen appeared, looking as if she were ready to join in the tears.

"What can we tell her that would possibly help?" Selena shook her head sympathetically, and gestured toward the caravan she now shared with her granddaughter. "This is her life now, and with no warning. She has lost everything. There is nothing to say. We can only be here to support our new sister." She paused, "How are preparations coming for the bonfire?"

Perry smiled, "Pretty well. The guys are building a fire break in the field where those farmers left. It's too bad. They could have had a good crop this year, I think. Hey," he interrupted himself, "did you all know that reinforcements were already here? I just met two of them, Patricia and Helen,

I think their names were. They said they were waiting for somebody to arrive this afternoon." With that, he hailed Quinsey and they went off in the direction of the farm.

"I don't like the sound of that," Gwen observed. "Meeting who?"

"I heard about this from Lorenzo," Selena replied. "It is a very sad case. You will see."

"Lorenzo is here? Really?" Gwen nearly danced with joy. "Oh, tonight will be perfect! When can we tell Karina? Maybe the idea of a party will cheer her up a little. Oh, wait 'til she hears Lorenzo sing!"

Selena placed a motherly arm around Gwen's shoulder. "I don't think it will help very much. This morning, when she mentioned that her womanly time had not yet come, I had to tell her …"

Gwen looked over at Karina's shaking form. "Oh …"

Selena nodded. "That was the breaking point."

It had been devastating news. While Karina had never made plans for children, hearing that all hope of bearing her own had gone was indeed the final straw. It didn't matter that she'd had no real hopes beyond Simon—and that set her off into a fresh round of agony—or that she'd told herself that later in her life would be better. The awful, cold reality of it was as bad as the bite that had cost her all the rest of her former life.

Gwen wrapped her arms around herself. "I'm not sure I have ever gotten over that myself."

"I know that you haven't," Selena smiled gently. "I know."

"Aren't we supposed to be stronger than this, though?" Gwen asked.

"According to whom?" Selena moved to the fire to retrieve the coffee pot and bring the ongoing needed boost of more hot caffeine to her granddaughter. "Why not see if you can help Sayuri hunt for dinner? Tonight's burning will be cathartic, if nothing else."

Well, Gwen went to her caravan, checked her supply of arrows and pulled her bowstring taut, ready for whatever game might appear. *If nothing else, I suppose it will be.*

"Send your pack away," Adam ordered. The stench was gagging him and his eyes watered as he held the rifle on his quarry.

"You are not in the position to order anyone to do anything," Vertigo almost simpered the words.

The two adversaries' attendants, some in gray, the rest in various filthy rags, had all stepped back to form a circle, eyeing one another with extreme disgust. Each tramp and Hunter was imagining a particularly enjoyable demise for the other—the Firewolves having the upper hand in every possible way.

"We only have a day," Adam began. "You and I both want desRosiers. Which of us is he coming after, I wonder? Why don't we both bring him in?"

"We don't need you for that," hissed Vertigo. "I have it on

good authority that there is a highly dissatisfied associate of desRosiers who will help me do just that."

They eyed one another.

Vertigo continued, "So why should I assist you?"

"Because, Padre," sneered Adam, and watched Vertigo stiffen his spine, "I know all about you is why. And I also know what actual name goes with that title. Third time's the charm, right?" He laughed heartily. "Let me know when you are ready to continue this conversation, all right?" Somebody snarled.

"All right," Vertigo raised a hand and his crew relaxed. "Leave us," he commanded, and the Firewolves melted into the brush. "Out of earshot!" There was a little more rustling, and the woods fell silent.

"Everyone. You, too," Adam ordered his Hunters. They scuffled away, a great deal more noisily and, quite enthusiastically, much farther.

"You seem different," the ancient werewolf's eyes burned into Adam's with all the fire of the underworld.

Vertigo waited until the last of the footsteps faded.

"Now. Speak to me ... my son."

Nessun Dorma

In the late afternoon, the day before the first night of the full moon, three Chimerae scouts were discussing the protection of the field from intruders.

"Intruders like what?" Perry was disappointed to be excluded from the evening's festivities, but accepted it as he shouldered his quiver. "Waltzing woodchucks?"

"Disco caterpillars?" offered Helen, adjusting her arrows and testing her bow.

Selena just shook her head and smiled. "You had plenty of fun the last time. Oh, Patricia; I hear your package arrived safely. Is everything settled?"

Patricia nodded, aiming a perfect shot at a passing rabbit. "Greg knows about it. Right now, it's, um, hidden in the woods and will stay there until he picks it up tomorrow." She strolled over to the fresh kill and put it into a pouch secured around her waist. "Lunch," she smiled.

"I don't really care for that arrangement," frowned Selena, "but under the circumstances, I cannot think of another way. Be aware of Vertigo, please. Even in human form he is formidable."

She wished the team luck and waved them toward their posts.

"All right. But if anything looks as if it's having more fun than I am—I don't care what it is—it's tomorrow's dinner," declared Perry, but he was cheerful enough as the trio headed off in separate directions.

Selena surveyed the field. Tanis's vardo had been destroyed with wild energy and a sense of glee by the men who'd been held in check by her thrall bite. Their awareness of what had become of them was sinking in fairly hard, and their pent-up destructive impulses were surging.

They were ultimately Selena's responsibility, and she allowed them full expression of their frustrations. Between their pain and Karina's, tonight's gathering might take some of the edge away, for a few hours at least.

The results of the spirited caravan demolition were stacks of well-splintered wood. The erstwhile thralls had placed these in the field within a series of creatively designed fire breaks (or "crop circles" as Gwen liked to call them), awaiting the arrival of their sister packs for a grand bonfire and dance.

It was a rare and unusual treat for the bloodlines to gather like this. In most cases, people didn't know one another's affiliations unless they were of the same pack; and of course, a pack was frequently made up of several bloodlines. As a security measure it seemed to work well, particularly for the Chimerae, who had managed to obscure their lineage through the ages. Tonight, they would be, simply, other werewolves.

Only Old Jake, whom everyone knew, was there to represent the Firewolves, but scores of members from every other bloodline who could make it would be in attendance. Early the next morning would see the Chimerae on their ways, far from the other wolves and the Hunter's plans. Selena worried that their absence would jeopardize their anonymity to a degree, but the pack had been unanimous about attending this night.

A joyous shout arose. To everyone's delight, Lorenzo had arrived at the gathering.

Gwen introduced him to Karina, who seemed quite taken with him. Her eyes still reddened, she distracted herself with opera talk. "Sorry. Classical music reminds me of my mother," she explained, as the tears began to form once more.

Lorenzo, who appeared to be in his early thirties, was full of humor and energy. He was an Earthwolf, he explained to her, and had been for about ten years. "Still new," he eyes danced, "but what it did for my voice! Ah! Aaaaaaaaaahh!" he sang a note, and everyone applauded.

"But you were a singer before!" protested Karina.

"Ah, yes; but now! Now I am a 'divo'!" He took Karina's hand and covered it with his own. "You will see, *carina mia*— you know your name in Italian, 'darling,' no?—you will sing tonight like a beautiful bird. Yes, yes, this I promise to you."

Karina's mood was lifted somewhat by the man's infectious energy. "Lorenzo, how can you get away with not singing in public on the full moon?"

"Well, you see," he led Karina back to the gathering group

of the bloodlines. "At first, you know, it was devastating. You know, of course," and he patted her hand. "But then you find ways, and for me, it was, you know, publicity. Good rumors, no?" With that, he bowed slightly, grinned and left her with Gwen. "Oh," he called over his shoulder, "I have one song just for you tonight, *carina mia!*"

Gwen was absolutely smitten, and her old flapper-girl self emerged with a sigh. "Oh, lucky you! Isn't he just the *berries*?"

Quinsey breezed by with some cushions. "Gwen's in loooooove!" she teased her friend. "Cradle robber!"

Karina allowed her mood to be uplifted by that of the others. Preparations were completed now, and the sun was low in the sky. Everyone had changed clothes, into the best of what they had, while the aroma of roasting venison added the final touches. There were fiddles, guitars, drums of various sizes, and other portable instruments, and someone had brought a flute.

Selena requested time to herself to oversee the bonfire. Karina caught some words in Ojibwe, but couldn't quite understand, though the significance was clear enough.

Once Selena returned, she seemed much more composed, and handed each of the three remaining men a torch. With the lighting of the huge bonfire, the party began to some lively bluegrass music and a large square dance. Greg was caller, and even Old Jake danced.

Karina watched Simon talking with a few of the other bloodline wolves. Her grandmother approached her softly.

"Our friend has looked after you well," she began, "and has kept his promises to me."

They found some cushions to sit on and continued their conversation as the music changed to an emotional Romani theme. Something about it brought the tears out again. Lorenzo, catching her eye, raised his hand as the last of the bright music faded, and all was still.

"For our newest cousin," Lorenzo bowed to Karina, "one sad song. Only one, and then, again we dance!"

The stars were just coming into their own as Lorenzo began the haunting aria *Una Furtiva Lagrima*, and anyone so inclined allowed his or her own tears to fall. The tenor's voice was indeed the most beautiful anyone there had ever heard, and everyone was tacitly permitted to employ that as an excuse for the emotions that swept through the large group and left a quiet pause before someone started clapping.

"Come, now!" After a standing ovation, Lorenzo bowed again and invited them all to sing. "You know this one—if you do not know it, sing the la-la-la," and everyone laughed. "And if you do not know the la-la-la, then you must waltz!"

With that, he began a rousing *Brindisi*, as Quinsey joined in followed by two dozen sopranos, basses and everything in between.

"Try!" Gwen shouted to her as she waltzed by in Carl's arms.

"Go on," coaxed Selena, and Karina could not believe what she was able to produce. She stood, overcome by it, and sang at the top of her lungs, her rich contralto adding to the chorus. Lorenzo swept her up in the waltz, still singing, and the night turned to a magical blend of colors, swirling dancers, and leaping firelight.

She briefly caught sight of Simon, who had joined her grandmother on the cushions, but pushed that from her mind. Presently, everyone was applauding again and asking for an encore.

"One moment, one moment," begged Lorenzo, feigning breathlessness as he deposited Karina back to her place, where she collapsed, exhausted yet invigorated, onto the cushions next to Selena. Simon was nowhere to be seen now, and Karina tried not to feel the sudden empty space. "Is this a regular thing?" she asked Selena.

"Not really," smiled her grandmother. "But from time to time, if the packs find themselves in the same area for one reason or another, we will reinforce our friendships."

"What brings the packs together?"

"In this case," Selena began slowly, "it is the upcoming battle with the Hunters."

"Where? At my place? At my house??" Karina shot upright. "I can help. Let me help!"

"Surrounded by enraged werewolves? Karina, you will be human. They would kill you. Think about that for a moment."

"I'll go tonight," Karina insisted, not hearing the warning. "There are how many, four left, Gwen said? Let me talk some sense into Adam. He will see reason; it's ridiculous!"

"I know about this Adam Hunter and why he is insane with revenge. Karina, even with only four of them, they have enough silver and enough hatred to eliminate all of our friends. They will not be dissuaded."

"So let me go! I can convince Adam, I know I can."

"Karina, you will not. All the Hunters need to do is stand their ground, inside your house. It will be that simple for them. They do not need your advice." A warning was growing in Selena's voice.

"Encore, encore!" shouted the crowd, as each chose a new partner and insisted that Lorenzo try to catch his breath a little faster.

"But—"

"Simon, would you stop lurking, please, and come over here?" Selena called over to Simon, who was pacing with increasing intensity about a hundred feet away.

"Simon," both women began at the same time.

"Karina, you'll stay with your pack." Simon's dark side was emerging again. "There is absolutely nothing you can do. Everything Selena has told you is true."

"Simon, one chance. Please."

Simon sat down. "Karina, you've had a lot of hard truth to deal with in the past few weeks, and I almost don't want to tell you this."

"Oh, try me."

"You know Adam's mission. You know what drives him. You must, must realize that you are now one of his targets."

Karina slumped.

"In daylight or on a non-crescent night, you can still be hurt badly, and those injuries will be what you live with every day for the rest of your life."

Selena nodded in agreement. "There is still so much for you to know, Karina. Adam will not hesitate to use you as bait again. Especially now. You are no longer human to him."

The hurt was unbearable. It wasn't only the inability to help; it was seeing her grandmother with Simon, these two old friends together. It was the echo of parental counsel when she brought home strays or ... or even on that night when she and Simon met. Karina looked at Selena and Simon as they watched her take it all in. The pain intensified as she felt her understanding of the bonds among the three of them shift. Simon had never been hers. Ever.

"I feel so helpless," was all she could muster.

It was Gwen and Quinsey who came to her rescue when they swept by and pulled her to her feet and into the next dance. "C'mon," whispered Gwen as they moved toward the circle, "it's going to be fine."

"It isn't."

Quinsey joined in with, "Karina, things look impossible right now. They might not be what they seem, though. Stick close, and you'll see."

"Feel that?" Gwen grinned. "Feel it? You know we sweep each other into the same mood, don'tcha? Well, just watch!" She swirled away, and Quinsey paused to allow Karina to catch up with that new spoonful of information.

"Breathe, honey," Quinsey said quietly. "Feel it now? Come on, you'll cheer up in no time, I promise."

Karina took a few deep breaths.

"That's it, that's right!" Quinsey encouraged her. "You'll learn to control your feelings, too, but for now, let's have some fun!"

By the early hours, the music had covered nearly every genre known to man and wolf. Simon and Karina peeled off by themselves, Karina reassuring him that she would stay put and that she was coming to grips with her new situation.

"I'm learning to handle a bow and arrow," she tried to laugh. "And to ride a motorbike. It's like having sisters. I've never had sisters. We even celebrate the moon cycle."

Simon's forced smiles and nods were of little comfort.

"Once I get back home, I'll have a whole new dimension to my artwork," she added, but Simon's expression had clouded, and he took her hand gently.

"Rina, you can't. Not just tomorrow. You can't go back at all."

"Of course I can! Nobody will know. How could they know?"

The silence was awful.

Karina stammered, "But my work, all my art, my house ..."

Simon kept her hand in his. "Selena will have some ideas

about all that. For now, she's taking you with the pack to Santa Fe, until you get used to this." He didn't know for how long that might be, but he promised this was the start of something new for her and that it wasn't necessarily the end of the road for her dreams. That comment hurt, and she wondered if he knew it, but she allowed him to draw her back into the wolf circle.

The first faint glow of a new day heralded the end of the night's revelry. "A finale, a finale!" begged the crowd, as they all mingled, hugged and said their parting words to one another.

"You know, *the* finale!" Gwen's voice rose above the others.

Simon placed his hands on Karina's shoulders and pressed his forehead to hers. "Breathe deep, and remember me." And with a final, deep look, he stepped back and took her hand again before disappearing into the darkness. Karina stood riveted. This was surely the end of something; at least goodbye for a long while.

Everyone stood in a ring facing the fire, as Lorenzo took the stage, such as it was. "All right, *the* finale." He blew a kiss to Gwen and she melted on the spot.

"'None shall sleep,' says this song, and so, we have not slept!" His words were greeted with a cheer. "My dearest friends, my companions, my blood cousins. *Nessun Dorma.*"

His voice rose with the early sun's rays, powerful and full.

One by one, each added a voice until the last note, which the Four Bloodlines held longer and more beautifully than was humanly possible: "*Vincero.*"

BLESS MY SOUL

Adam trained his pistol on the disgraced Padre Vicente Marquez, exiled priest of Old Spain, as the latter waved away a cloud of flies that had surrounded his face.

"Truce," sneered the werewolf. "Perhaps in spite of all that you have learned of us, Hunter, you are not yet aware that we cannot be killed by a mere bullet? Even in human form."

"I know all about it. It would sure slow you all down, though."

"Let us stop this posturing," Marquez motioned Adam to a seat on a nearby log. "We are better fighters than you in either shape, and we will surely kill you. This truth is simple, isn't it, really? Even to your exhausted, bottle-clouded eyes?"

Adam's indignant sniff ended the discussion. Declining the seat and leaning against a tree, he spat violently.

"Of course," continued Marquez with a chilling smile, "you have taken your share of my people, too. Especially the new ones; they never can control it, can they? They believe themselves to be unconquerable and they fall to the silver bullet. So tell me, young Hunter, what has driven you to chase me down?"

Adam aimed his pistol between the scruffy tramp's eyes and snarled, "You know damn well why. I want desRosiers. Here's what's in it for you. My men and I leave you and yours alone and you all ignore us. You have all the fun you want with whatever the hell is coming in the next few days. We'll dive in only when and if it's appropriate. Simple truth." He cocked the hammer. "And I don't care that this won't kill you but it will knock you into next week. And it'll take the edge off a hell of a lot, as far as I'm concerned."

Marquez waved a filthy hand. "I believe you, my son."

"And knock that off." Adam waved the firearm. "You lost that privilege three centuries or so ago."

"Yes …" mused the werewolf, an odd light burning in his eyes. "And how, again, do you know this?"

"Same way you know me, I guess." Adam shifted his weight against the tree, keeping his pistol at the ready.

"I know that your family has been chasing us for at least a hundred years," began Marquez.

"Oh, at least."

"I know this because I have now based myself near Austin."

"Back near home—near Austin?" Adam challenged him, "Why come back to Austin?"

Marquez shrugged. "Because Austin is … weird. Enough for us, at any rate. We are lately to be found in the Balcones Canyonlands."

"Then it's more than being drawn to your territory." Adam

stood up fully. "Isn't it."

"We are attached to places." *And sometimes to people.* Marquez looked furtively toward his group, whom he could still hear in the woods guarding against the return of Adam's men. He called out, "Leave them be, leave it all. Go. Find something to do."

Two of the shabby creatures exchanged hideous grins as they ran past and left the Firewolf camp at top speed, and Adam caught the words "two or three of them hunting rabbits nearby."

Marquez turned his attention back to Adam. "Yes. Perhaps more than that. The impulses, the connections, they cannot always be controlled. But you? I am so very curious as to how you know my name, specifically."

You're joking. Adam stared at him.

"You really don't know," he said aloud. "You have personally tormented my family for centuries and you really don't know."

"I knew of your grandfather. I knew of your great-grandmother, a Huntress too; though I see that information surprises you. But my name …" something dawned in Marquez's mind.

Adam watched the wheels turn in the werewolf's head. Flashes of his own past returned to him—his father calling him into the library to show him the two-hundred-fifty-year-old diary of his ancestor.

Vertigo took up the conversation. "You were, quite simply,

handy. You and your family would never leave the ranch you had built on my territory. But my name ...?" A disquieting thought persisted. During the migration, when they came to build the mission. With the train, there was a particularly sweet, bright convent girl. He could not stop himself. He'd called her over one brightly moonlit night to hear her confession. How softly her skin glowed. The half-moon was reflected in her trusting eyes. A very lovely girl, he remembered.

For his part, Adam's mind was back in the library once again, facing the rage of his father and father-in-law over the deaths of his wife and son the night before. He barely heard them, dumbstruck with sorrow and fury, resenting each word they shot at him. Adam had failed the Hunter name. He was to swear on the ancient diary. He was to raise a fresh generation of Hunters and track the beasts down while his own grief was powerful enough to drive him. *It will never go away. Not ever. Not. Even. Now.*

"You changed your name!" Vertigo stood, choking on his own shock. "You ... you are not named Hunter!"

"Not originally," Adam's cool demeanor had returned with him to the present. "You'll do what I ask and I'll tell you how to do it."

"I will, I will!" snarled the werewolf.

"I know your true name, Marquez, and I'll use it against you. Now hear mine, you perverted old goat. You remember that girl from Mexico City, the one you mistreated all the way up the *Camino Real de los Tejas* to the mission? She bore your child before you were bitten, and was cast out for it. Of course, after that you found her again. Went at her again, didn't you, in wolf form, though."

Vertigo shivered. "She lived? *She lived?*"

Adam nodded. "She lived. You got at her one more time, after she married the *granjero* who took her and the baby into his home. But she managed to survive the bite you gave her after you turned. Didn't know that? Really? Then you didn't know how much her husband loved her. The way I loved Mary Beth. After you bit her, he built her a cellar, to hide her there every full moon. She lived out her days quietly, and under the radar, except for the diary she left behind. Say it," Adam commanded. "For her memory's sake, say it and apologize. Say out loud the true name of my sixth-great grandmother. Say it, *Granddad!*"

FIRST NIGHT

Simon was about to put out the pack's First Night campfire and bury it in dirt. The rest of the men, most of them bare-chested and in oversized sweatpants, readied themselves for the coming night. "Has everybody eaten?" Simon called automatically before extinguishing the small fire.

A rustle sounded at the clearing's edge; they all wheeled, almost ferally, to face Greg. Along with him was what looked to be a five-foot bundle of clothes that clung to him.

Greg's words were lost behind an unearthly wail emerging from this small rag pile, and the group stopped, startled, upon meeting their new guest. Simon heard a heartbreaking, open-mouthed *"no no no"* as a slight girl fell sobbing to her knees, clutching at Greg's trouser legs, fighting all attempts to set her on her feet.

"Good lord, she is young," breathed Simon. The rest of the group moved forward slightly. "How did this happen to her? What is it? We're still human, and she's terrified of us."

"She was with a group of migrant workers right near the Texas border. She's the only one who survived it, but she did get the bite." Greg bent to speak softly to his companion, who only curled into a ball and dry-heaved. "It's the border-watchers' new trick. Find one or two of the Firewolves with no scruples, set 'em on a camp full of people, and that's the end of them. Unless of course, the Weirdos want toys to play with. She escaped that part, at least. She got bitten too close to dawn, and it seems the wolves lost her when they all scattered."

The group closed in, a half-dozen or so voices trying to soothe the youngster without knowing what to say. Most of them had run into their bitewolves as adults, the exception being Old Jake, who was staring and trembling, reliving some childhood horror or other. The fire began to crackle.

"This is Lucia. She's a little afraid of us, obviously, but I couldn't find Patricia or Helen tonight to look after her," Greg rose to his impressive height and swallowed hard. "Simon, how's your Spanish?"

"Uh, *mucho … malo*. Selena's is pretty good, though. I'll take her in once this cycle is over." *If we survive it.*

He squinted at the little form on the ground. "Jeez, what do we do? If we scare her *now* …"

"It's not that," responded Greg, lifting the girl to her feet and protecting her with a giant arm, swaying gently as she dug her fingernails into his pullover, "It's …" they could hardly hear him, "I can't convince her this isn't one of those *other* camps, you know …" he looked helpless, then snarled, as Lorenzo got a little too close, "She's fourteen!"

This sent them all into a rapid, silent retreat.

"What, a Hunters' camp?" Tyler spoke first, but it was Carl

who understood. "Christ." He shook his head. "Ah, Christ."

Greg enveloped his charge and addressed Tyler over her dark head, "The *coyotes*—the migrant smugglers—cull the youngest and prettiest and take 'em to the worker camps for … They …" no more was needed. The entire group of men fell uncomfortably silent.

Simon's eyes dropped and he would have given anything for a long and scalding shower. "I wish I didn't know that," he mumbled and the others echoed his feelings by shifting slowly away from their new charge and toward the woods.

"Has everybody eaten?" Greg asked suddenly, and four of the group reached for their stashed backpacks to produce a variety of sandwiches and fruit for the girl.

She accepted an apple from Tyler, who'd approached as if Lucia were a wild deer, and spoke softly, very softly, until the girl took it and he was able to step away from her.

The men had retreated by this time, all save Old Jake, who stared in wide-eyed recognition of a fellow child-wolf. Simon put an arm around Jake's shoulder and pulled him away. "This her first full cycle?"

"Yeah. They were attacked just before sunup, fifth night of the last moon, so she only got the tail end of it. I don't think she remembers much, but she knows what's happening."

"I'll explain everything to Selena."

"Was hoping you would, once she gets through this week. She'll be safe with them for a few days, and we'll pick her up again once she adjusts."

Sickened and embarrassed by the horror of what Lucia was afraid of, some of the men had put their T-shirts back on, and the adrenalin-infused activity of the camp had ceased.

Carl kept shaking his head, "And people worry about *us*." He looked skyward, "How long?"

"She'll go first," warned Greg, "So scatter at first sign. Lorenzo, you grab Old Jake, he's been tetchy these last two cycles. Tyler," he turned to the former forestry student, who had finished taking care of the campfire, "You go right now. I don't want either of you two newbies near each other."

"I've got him," Carl clapped Tyler on the back congenially and off they went.

"See you under the sun." The rest of the wolfmen slipped into the gloomy trees.

"How did you find her?" Simon stretched and flexed, feeling the first rush of the moon.

"Patricia and Helen brought her in through a contact, but I lost them yesterday. I don't know why they'd leave her like this." Greg shook his head, his eyes on Lucia. "Won't be long now. How long can you hold off?"

"I can hold the worst off for about ninety minutes."

"Lucia," Greg placed a huge hand on his new charge's shoulder. She looked up, calmer. Simon was struck by how very lovely she was. Greg spoke rapidly in Spanish and Lucia nodded, hiccupping. Turning her huge brown eyes to Simon, she whispered, "*Encantada*." Those eyes were beginning to show an outer ring of blue.

Simon smiled warmly, "My friend Selena will look after you soon." Greg translated; Lucia shuddered suddenly. "Hey, you better leave, Simon, you know how fast the cubs usually go."

Simon hesitated. "She hasn't eaten much. Can you hold her off on your own?"

"Sure—what are *you* gonna do?" Greg flashed a grin. "Hey; take a sec, catch her scent."

Simon leaned over and breathed deeply, watching anarchy slowly replace the fading moral conscience in Lucia's eyes. "OK, got her."

Greg continued, "I'll see her through this one. So now, you have her scent and my back, just in case she turns on one of us. Got it?"

Nodding, Simon took one last glance at the teen, whose face was now revealing the first signs of The Rush. It was catching, and Greg saw it in Simon's eyes. "*Go!*"

And Simon took off, exhilarated, unfettered, limbs lengthening uncomfortably, his bounding strides carrying his raspy-breathed form through the underbrush. It was only First Night, but the wolf was high in him, though not complete. A rabbit shot past him and he snapped at it gleefully, thrilling to its terror before getting a grip on himself. The Rush resurfaced presently, sending him hurtling through the woods to the spot where he scented the pack, all save Greg and Lucia, and he let out a mighty lung-tearing howl.

Someone, maybe Tyler, responded and he heard Old Jake

and Lorenzo in the distance. And then, just then, a new one, thin and pure, rose above the trees, and the entire pack responded in joyous unison to its newest sister under the moon.

The Promise

Simon and Old Jake lay in a small clearing, awash in the warm hues of dawn that fell in a low slant through the blue-gray trees. Last night they had come across the human-form bodies of Patricia, Perry, and Helen, who'd fallen victim to the horrors of the Firewolf gang before sunset. The images could not be shaken off by either of the men, and the terrified child Lucia was still on their minds.

"Simon," Jake shadowed his eyes from the sunlight and rolled over, concentrating on the dark earth.

"Simon," he said again, listening to his friend's rough breathing. "You seen the sun?"

"Yeah. I'm here."

"I can't do this anymore. *Simon.*"

Simon snapped into a seated position, staring at his friend.

"Simon, last night I saw there was some silver chains over a log in the woods."

"Yes, that's where—go on." Simon's gut twisted, and he started to get up.

"No, you don't, don't you go walking away from me," Jake growled. "Listen up, Simon. There's still a couple of them chains left. Tonight's the night we get Vertigo. I'll tell you how. Promise me."

The light was brightening, and they heard Greg call their names.

"I mean it, Simon. You fix me down somewhere good and tight with those chains near me tonight. That old dog comes for me and whoosh! We take him out for good."

Greg appeared. "Jake! You lucid?"

"No, he isn't!" Simon stared at his companion, who was still stretched out face down.

"Couple more minutes," Jake shivered slightly and covered his eyes. "I can't do it anymore. Tell everyone I'm done, boys. Vertigo will come at me with his old tricks and I'll take him out at exactly the same time I go. It'll be the last thing I do and I'll rest easy. Give me that much, boys. Promise me."

Simon exhaled. "Jake, we're all in this together. We aren't going to—"

Jake buried his head in his arms. "You'll do it. We'll get him for sure this way. Let me do this one thing."

Simon shook his head violently, "Not a chance. I'm not killing you."

The light was overcoming the night's shadows.

"Do this for me," Jake looked up and at him directly as the blue rings faded. "No matter how much I beg you to let me go," he laughed, "just like in the old fairytales."

"I'll do it," Greg promised softly, and Simon stared at him.

"Good. Don't let me down. I'd do it myself, you know I

would if I could. But if I have your help, we can get him for sure. Gregory, tell him. Tell him, Gregory! Gregory! Seen the sun?" and Old Jake rolled in the dirt, laughing like a four-year-old who had just discovered the joys of playing in the mud.

Greg and Simon exchanged dark looks.

"You're kidding. Right?" Simon watched Greg sit down and cover his face with his hands for a moment.

"You're *kidding* me!" Simon said again. "That's like murdering a toddler!"

Greg looked up and stared him down. "It wasn't the child who asked. It was the man."

Simon stretched out on his back, soaking in the sunlight and listening to Old Jake run back and forth trying to catch a butterfly.

"I'm not doing this."

"You don't have to. I gave him my word. Shut up, Simon," it was Greg's turn to sit up straight. Simon swallowed hard and waited for his old friend to continue.

"Look," Greg continued, "how tired are you after seventy-some years of this? How do you think I feel? You think the last two hundred years of immortality and chasing squirrels has been fun? You think I haven't considered a way out? I have sat in the woods with a silver coin, just waiting for the sun to set. No, you didn't know that, did you?"

Simon sat down and stretched his arms out across his bent knees, looking past Greg and toward Jake's merry game. "That kind of thing wouldn't be right, either, Chief," he said quietly.

"I don't give a flying damn what you think is right." Greg stood up and began pacing. "You tell me you haven't thought about it."

Simon looked down, guiltily.

"We all have. But here's the difference about tonight. We're losing this game, Simon; between Hunters and Fire-wolves, we're losing it. You know there haven't been enough of us in any of the gatherings. But tonight, with the Hunters down so many, we have a real chance of concentrating on the Firewolves and taking out Vertigo. Once he goes, the rest scatter."

"Take out Vertigo on a suicide mission. That's your plan. Why? We need all of us, if you're going to be so damn practical."

"We're it, Simon. There aren't many of us left, if you can consider us the good guys. Who did we lose last night? Do you even know? Between Hunters and Firewolves, we are down by fourteen, Simon. Half of them were newbies. Fourteen! There are only four Hunters, and we were on the run the whole time.

"Vertigo is letting the Hunters take over and do his dirty work for him, so he and the other Firewolves can regroup and take over. They form their own kingdom of thralls and heaven have mercy on the human race."

"C'mon, don't be so dramatic. The Chimerae are on our side."

"Sure, let's let our friends do this on our behalf. Selena could handle it, obviously. She did a great job two weeks ago, in spite of the fact that she hates hunting humans. But she did it. So sure, why not let her."

"And this is the best you can come up with!" Simon exploded.

"Simon. This may be the first you've heard of it but it is not the first time Jake has asked me for this." Greg's jaw was clenched and he stared into the woods. "Far from it!"

Old Jake came scampering back, wide-eyed, looking from one to the other like a child watching his parents fight.

"It's all right, Jake." Simon shaded his eyes as he looked up at the old man.

"Oh, no it ain't," Greg declared softly. Then he stood and walked back into the woods to find the silver-laced log.

Lycanthropic Blues

The day after his bite, a barely contained Adam had installed himself in the guest house. It was mostly for privacy, and also to think up new plans, he had told the Hunter trio, whom he had come to think of, with a complete lack of affection, as the Three Stooges.

And for the love of all that was holy, they were to clean the place up in case Karina showed up again and wanted her house back. Dishwashing began immediately. The Stooges exchanged mutinous looks as Adam vacated Karina's place and headed for the log cabin.

Adam's move to Simon's former quarters had been the ideal cover for the remaining crescent moon phase. He had been able to get away, silently, for his nightly morphing, the guest house being far enough out of the way to provide undetectable travel. No wonder it had worked so efficiently for desRosiers.

The silver threads that graced the guest house bedroom created a few odd vibrations, like a very mild electric current, so at least he knew what to avoid there if he somehow ended up back here in wolf form. The damn stuff worked, though.

That was something, at least.

He had taken all possible steps to protect his new identity. Apparently, there was nothing else to worry about, he thought wryly as he passed a mirror in the hallway.

He'd heard nothing more than an acknowledgement from the FBI after reporting Reese missing this morning, the first after the full moon cycle, and he wasn't about to start them off on a hunt of their own. He still wasn't sure about the extent of what they knew about the Chimerae.

Managing the cycle on his own had been agony, though. He had been able to contain the loudest of his howls and to stay far from humans, though his appetite had grown ravenous. During the day it was bad enough, but at sunset! The morning after the Crescent Moon, he'd awakened next to the carcass of a half-gutted stag, his shredded sweatshirt soaked in blood and gore.

The scent had attracted a large prowling bear who was eager to feed her two cubs that morning. One snarl and a glare from the human Adam, and the animals retreated in haste.

A pale ray of light illuminated the blood on his hands, and some piece of advice or other drifted into his memory, something about … ah, yes. He crawled away from the deer, and into a small patch of sunlight where he lay on his back and drank in the morning sun. Yes, that was it. You have to see the sun.

A sudden distaste overwhelmed him. He smelled the waters of the frigid creek nearby and plunged into its icy current, washing off the night's kill. He pulled off what was left of his sweatshirt and watched it rush away downstream. No shirt next time, he noted. For curiosity's sake, he tried to track his path back to the guest house, but he didn't find anything to add to his knowledge.

For the first time, back at the house, he wondered how the Howlers controlled the raging animal aspect of their being. Last night, Adam's fury was unbridled, but he knew from experience that Howlers weren't always that carried away. Was this why they traveled in packs? Did they police one another? How did they contain the thirst for blood? Did they talk about it much?

He shook his head angrily. What, was he getting soft? Did he forget his purpose here?

The only good discovery was that of his heightened senses. He would know when anything was approaching, and what form it took, either from its sound or by the way its scent carried on the breeze. Even his eyesight was much sharper. For his own amusement and discovery, he'd tacked a magazine cover to the wall fifteen feet away and was able to read every letter on it.

Adam's renewed feelings of vengeance had been overshadowing an emerging and not unwelcome truth. All of this, every aspect of it, he could use. He would pour it into his continued hunt for desRosiers.

The Howler fight was not over for him. Not by a long shot. After all, who, except maybe the FBI's cryptozoology team, believed in the Chimerae? Even if they did, who would suspect a Hunter, who was immune to the death sting of silver and in full human form under the full moon?

It was all unfolding to him. He would protect the secret of the Chimerae, and in doing so could completely cover his new identity. Even if the Chimerae themselves discovered the truth, why would they tell?

There was one more glimmer of light in his new situation. There was no longer an immediate rush to find and end desRosiers. He essentially had forever.

Full moon was now approaching. He wondered who would get the last howl in.

SALVATION

O nce his mind cleared, Simon wondered how he couldn't
have seen the obvious solution to saving Jake and
keeping the promise after all.

Skirting the town, he ran across a moving van parked
down a long driveway with its tailgate unlocked. Evidently
after the past month's almost incessant racket in the woods,
the last of the locals had just jumped in their cars and left
everything. Around the vehicle were several containers of
gasoline, water, and other travel necessities. He soon found
what he needed, and armed with two cans of motor oil, he
headed back for the encampment.

There wasn't much point in hiding his tracks, since by
now, everybody knew where everyone else was lurking. The
remaining Hunters were at Karina's battered house, Simon
and company were three miles in the woods to the west, and
the Firewolves were camped two miles to the east of them.

Simon and Greg had an idea that they might join forces
with the Hunters for one night to take down the Firewolves,
but when they approached the house, Adam and his idiots put
paid to that with a couple of badly aimed rifle shots that flew

past their ears.

In a little over an hour, Simon had returned to camp, treasures in hand.

"Hey, Jake!" Simon called out as he approached the tent where Greg and the old man were resting. "I brought you something!"

"A present? A present!" Jake appeared, grinning, Greg on his heels.

"Well, yeah; sort of a strange present," Simon placed the cans on top of a rock.

"Jake," he began, "you know how you hate silver? I think I have something that will protect you."

The plan dawned on Greg immediately. Jake took a moment, the familiar scent of motor oil penetrating his memory.

He panicked.

"He' here!" and Old Jake burst into tears. "It' Vertigo. Coming to get me! Help me, Simon! He' gonna get me again!"

"Shhhhh," soothed Greg. "Jake, listen up. I know what Simon's thinking. He is going to put the motor oil on you so that when you hold the silver it won't hurt you."

"I don't wanna hold silver!" Jake hiccupped. But something was stirring in his mind. "Don't wanna go like Jimmy."

"I know!" Simon smiled. "And you won't, see? We'll put this on you, watch, just like this ... here, wait! Simon says, we'll put this on you. See? There. And you can hold the silver. Any silver. I think you asked Greg to give you some silver tonight." Simon wasn't at all sure how far he could press his friend's broken memory.

The wheels were turning in Jake's fragmented thoughts. As Simon turned away to open the other oil can, the old werewolf's expression seemed to clear. He turned to Greg and they whispered a rapid conversation. Greg nodded.

"What was that?" Simon asked sharply.

"We'll do it your way," Greg replied. He turned and strode away into the woods.

"Great," Simon grinned with relief. Happily, he pulled Old Jake over to the rock. Sundown was less than fifteen minutes away now. "Come on, Jake, let's put this on you. I mean, Simon says ... let's put this all over you." Simon bent to help him oil up.

Jake bowed his head and gazed down at Simon; then he lightly placed a hand on his longtime friend's head. Simon looked up at him with a smile and responded, "There, not so bad, is it?"

Old Jake shook his head and sat down on the rock, breathing deeply.

Greg reappeared, taking Simon aside and speaking softly. "Now that you know the bones of the plan, here's the rest. Firewolves are already on the way. They're going to intercept us just about sunset, so come out clawing, wild as you can. I don't know where Hunter's fools went but I think the others from our collective are leading them on a chase. Vertigo is coming to claim Jake."

"How did you get him to do that?"

"Same thing I told you, only from a distance," Greg grinned. "I talked to him yesterday morning."

"You what?"

"This has been coming for a while, Simon. Jake and I have it covered." Greg could hardly look at the pain of betrayal in Simon's eyes.

"I told Vertigo I was tired of it all. Said I was sick of you and your virtuous ways." *Why did there seem to be a grain of truth in that?* "Told him I was striking off on my own," Greg continued. "That he should come take his little toy and go. Then I told him where we'd be."

"And he believed you? He didn't scent the lie, coming from the best lie detector in the woods?"

"Nope." Greg picked up the chain in a thickly gloved hand and nodded. "Ready? You, Jake? Are you ready?" Jake looked up. Looking deeply into Greg's eyes and swallowing hard as the big man offered him a jelly candy from his pocket, Jake accepted the other glove and chain. His eyes were ringed already as his bitewolf rapidly approached.

Greg and Simon stepped away from him, keeping their eyes on Jake and their backs to the setting sun in a heroic last-minute exercise of self-control. "Remember to let go fast and hard," hissed Greg.

Jake turned to face them and the fiery sunset, giving Simon an oddly clear look. "Good night, Simon," he smiled as he trembled violently once more. The smile turned to a fanged howl as Jake turned wolf with the final rays of sunlight.

Simon and Greg morphed right behind him, twisting and shrieking as Vertigo landed at their feet, snarling at the chain in Jake's still gloved hand.

Now fully focused, Simon was overcome by Jake's composure as Vertigo crouched and slavered, aware of the silver weapon. In a fantastic twirl, Vertigo made an expertly calculated lunge just past Jake and attacked from behind. Escaping the silver's burn, he took Jake's gloved forearm clean off, sending it and the chain flying across the clearing.

At the same instant, Jake spun to face Vertigo, bent over his bitewolf and held him tightly with his other arm.

In two nearly simultaneous flashes, both wolves immolated.

On the other side of the clearing lay the chain and Jake's withered wolf arm, which was rapidly disintegrating.

At the place where Old Jake and Vertigo had flashed into eternity dropped Greg's silver coin. It hung in midair a brief moment, then fell from precisely the spot it had been in Jake's throat, partially encased in the melted jelly he had swallowed just before sunset. The coin had immolated Jake from the inside out. As it dropped, in a flash of unforeseen and absolute justice, it destroyed el Padre Vicente Marquez, his demonic tormentor.

Greg and Simon howled in unison, watching the space where the two wolves had existed a second before. Simon shrieked in rage, Greg in grief. "*I promised the man,*" Greg's words bounced back into Simon's brain. The chief had taken no chances.

There was no time left. Simon and Greg heard the screaming howls as Vasquez and Harris met their bitewolves and their instant transformation.

The two newly minted Firewolves were on Simon and Greg in seconds, with their bitewolves hot on their heels. The attackers all leaped the rock into the clearing; three hit the messy lines of silver chains while one skidded into the half-hidden silver coin. Four flashes erupted into silence.

Greg and Simon, unscathed but eyes burning, high-tailed it back toward Karina's cottage. Two Hunters down, and two to go, never mind what would happen to Simon and Greg when the Firewolves began to realize that their king was gone forever.

Simon picked up Adam's scent first, and veered toward the guest house. Something wasn't right about it, but in his maddened state, he refused to see it. He paused long enough to see Greg's prey, Jones, meet his death at the hands of the fully enraged Earthwolf, whose furiously slashing claws and vicious jaws tore into him and sent pieces of the Hunter in every direction. Not even the presence of silver could overcome Greg's madness. Simon wondered how likely it was that Greg deeply wanted to join his old friend in sweet oblivion tonight.

He flinched at the drip of warm blood that slid from the branch above, kissed the back of his neck and ran like a wet tongue down his spine in the leafy darkness. Jones's Hunters patch stung his eyes as it hung there, and it was a small miracle that Simon missed brushing up against it. Heaven knew how Greg had managed to survive it.

The Earthwolf chief's infuriated howls had alerted Adam to their encroaching presence. In a moment or two, he emerged onto the porch, immediately aiming in Simon's direction.

How could he have known exactly where Simon was, when Greg was right there in all his Technicolor werewolf rage? Simon knew he couldn't get to the Hunter in time to disarm him and quickly scanned out an escape route. He saw a clear path in the two hundred yards back where he'd come from, between the trees, their dismembered human fruit dripping red juice into slickened roots.

Greg had already taken off at an astonishing speed into the woods to defend the remaining members of his own pack from Firewolves.

Of the three sets of enemies who began this night, Adam was the last Hunter left alive. He moved slowly down the steps and into the yard, listening, tasting the air, straining all of his newly-honed senses to pick up a whiff of full-moon Howler.

Simon hesitated. Something was off. Adam didn't smell right.

Simon backed into the trees slowly, circling the Hunter, and maneuvered until he was at his prey's back. Adam seemed uncharacteristically confused, so Simon began dogging him from about ten yards, hardly breathing, blocking his retreat to the cabin. He watched Adam take in the gory remnants of

Jones.

Adam whirled and shot.

Simon dodged the splattering silver, lunging to the side and into the trees, making a beeline for the deep woods.

Adam was beginning to feel like himself again. His silver-stitched Hunters patch caught the moonlight. The rifle tingled in his hands. He hitched the belted string of wolf ears to his left. His way was clear, but he had heard the unmistakable growl of the beast nearby and knew the Howler was faster than he could ever be in his current form. Nevertheless, he paused to check his rifle, then ran for it. He could get to the Morris house for cover and more ammo. They had extra pieces of silver around for just this purpose, the Diner Ladies did. He remembered their honest faith in the Hunters, and his resolve became superhuman.

Simon padded along the Hunter's direction, keeping by the roadside. He suddenly realized where Adam was headed, and beat him to it, unbolting the front door to the Morris house with an elongated clawed hand, hurling himself inside and diving into the living room corner, deep under the torn-up sofa where one of the Diner Ladies had met an unspeakable end. Adam followed seconds later, trembling, heaving deeply and noisily, absorbing what he thought was safety.

In the blackness, Simon controlled his breathing, amazed still at the humanity he retained in spite of the moon and his attendant rage. Nevertheless, memories of the night's most precious victim raised his hackles; he suppressed a shudder, but could not control the growl.

Adam's hair stood on end and he went cold, down to his toenails. He crept toward the corner; slowly he raised the gun with its single silver bullet—his last. One shot would be enough. All it had to do was touch the beast to engulf it in flames. The range was so close. He heard the shuffling in the corner under the sofa and knew where to aim. He could blind desRosiers with a burst from his high-beam flashlight if he could just get to it with his free hand.

Simon upended the sofa and pounced as the ultra-white beam of light lit a fairground hell-house scene of tilted furniture and spilling knickknacks, sending shadows up the walls like so many large black spiders. Adam fired and missed, rolling out of Simon's way as the silver bullet melted from the friction and dripped down the wall. Decades of someone's personal accumulations crashed out of an upended chest, which now blocked the direction of Adam's escape. The flashlight was knocked out of his reach and landed between two cushions, its beam focused upward. Adam slid under an armchair and curled up as much as he could to protect his vulnerable throat. He forced himself to remember that now, a bite elsewhere would simply wound him. He pushed such an injury's very real permanence out of his imagination. Simon stood erect, eyes burning, howling to the rooftop.

The burst of light had imprinted the Hunters patch onto Simon's retinas, engulfing his sanity and sending him into a near mythical lycanthropic rage. He recoiled, and another piece of furniture next to the sofa spilled open, sending old china figurines and a collection of ugly ceramics crashing downward. The flashlight was shifted again, painfully illuminating a bright splash of coins from a shattered yellow piggy bank. At the same instant, Adam and Simon saw the pieces of silver. Adam reached from under the armchair, and Simon lurched backwards. Adam laughed brutally, and with both hands scooped the silver coins and aimed. It would take only one to make contact, and they both knew it. Simon twisted away from Adam's hands, bared his fangs, lunged forward and bit deep into the Hunter's leg.

Adam threw the coins just as sunrise pierced the living room windows.

Dawn appeared gently. No birds sang, and animals were eerily silent.

Slowly a single figure approached the Morris house, recording device in hand, his eyes focused on the lone Hunter who leaned pale and exhausted against an abandoned car at the end of the driveway.

The Hunter stood to his full height, his tattered jacket telling a part of the previous night's story. He led the reporter up the steps, opened the front door, and encouraged the valiant *Creek Run* reporter to look inside at the scattered coins. "I think we got him."

The reporter recorded the moment for the absentee residents of Pigeon Creek, sure of his Pulitzer now.

"I'll do one final check for Howler sign." The last remaining Hunter waved off the reporter's questions and strode bravely off into the wild, wooded land beyond the little town.

The reporter was taking notes when he thought he heard a noise coming from inside the Morris house. Cautiously, emboldened by the coming daylight, he peered into the upended mess, but saw and heard nothing more. He stepped in, picked up a few of the scattered coins and examined the dates; only a few of them were old enough to contain silver. Just one was all it took, wasn't it? Of course, if it hadn't hit the beast ...

The reporter strained to hear anything more but couldn't bring himself to linger in the room. Like everyone else, he'd spent his mornings in the diner and had been fond of its owners.

Was something moving under that blanket? Trick of the light, it had to be. The reporter shivered, closed the front door and walked back to his car, deep in thought. Adjusting the rear-view mirror, he paused and took a look, shook his head, and turned on the ignition. Time to head to his office. He had a news outlet to run, after all. Nobody else was going to do it. One more glance into the mirror, and he saw the blanket spill out of the front door, down the steps, and roll to the curb. *Hmm. Must have dislodged it. Couldn't have closed the door properly.* Convinced, almost, he floored the gas pedal and raced back to the *Creek Run* office, sparing himself the sight of the blanket rising and staggering toward the bushes.

About a mile into the woods, Simon picked up Greg and the remaining wolfmen and shucked Adam's ill-fitting Hunter's jacket.

"What's this?" asked the great Earthwolf, kicking it aside.

"I'll explain it all after breakfast," responded Simon. "For now, let's call it Karma."

Hunter and Chimera though he was, it took nearly a month of expert searching for Adam to locate the now-deserted summer camp of the Chimerae. He'd abandoned his car once it ran out of gas, and had more or less surrendered to the wild side of himself. His crescent cycle was punctuated by two more large kills before he realized that filling his stomach before sunset, as he had seen Simon do, was the solution to that part at least.

Karina's scent still lingered there, powerful in the new-moon nighttimes when he snuffled and growled through the partially empty vardos. He ought to find them, he thought. Selena would help. Surely Karina would have some compassion? He caught a whiff of stale paints near the caravan she had shared with Selena and whimpered a little.

"Welcome to the club," desRosiers had snorted upon realizing that his Waterwolf bite had not taken hold in the pre-dawn moments of that final struggle. Maybe Simon was right about joining a pack, but one that was far, far away. He'd warned Adam not to pursue Karina and her grandmother, but what did he know? Vertigo was gone. The Hunters were finished. Adam ought to give it all up, join Selena's Chimera pack, and forget about desRosiers, but the memories of all he had lost were too powerful. Yes. He needed nobody. He was Adam Hunter. He had to do this for the honor of Mary Beth and his little son. His nearly invisible form stood tall in the black Minnesota night and emitted a fierce growl.

He had his own pack to re-form now. He needed new Hunters.

EPILOGUE

Creek Run Dispatch: Normalcy returns to Pigeon Creek

Pigeon Creek—In spite of the unusually heavy snow this year, the past few months have seen many residents slowly returning to our little town to resettle.

After a long and thorough investigation, law enforcement has uncovered no further leads in the disappearance of artist Karina Redfeather or her cousin, Simon desRosiers. A spokesperson who wished to remain anonymous said that the discovery over the summer of Redfeather's shredded clothing and a massive quantity of dried blood indicated that she may no longer be alive.

Whether or not desRosiers is a suspect is still unclear.

Former Sheriff *pro tem* Adam Hunter has resigned and returned to Texas. The disappearance of his colleagues has not been fully explained, but it is reported that Hunter has continued to work with the FBI as they continue their investigation.

Sheriff Langston has returned to temporary duty until his retirement in two more months. A special election will take place in three weeks.

Residents are invited to pay their respects this Thursday afternoon as we commemorate the renaming of our main thoroughfare as "Hunter's Road" in memory of the missing. Light refreshments will be served and a moment of silence will be held.

No further leads seem available in the apparently related murders of our Diner Ladies last summer, but a new special agent with the FBI released a statement in September to the effect that the killer or killers no longer presented a threat and that Pigeon Creek was perhaps safer than almost any other town in the Minnesota woods.

On that safety note: The Hillstrom family reports that there was some sort of large animal roaming around near the Redfeather property last night, but as it was a new moon, they could not identify what it was. A heavy snow overnight wiped out any tracks that it might have left.

Residents are reminded that this winter has been difficult and that they should keep trash bins locked up to deter prowling beasts.

###

Addenda: Notes and approaches

Monsters have walked among us since the first humans looked up at the phases of the moon. Of course, stories of shapeshifters, werewolves, catwomen, and other such creatures have sprung up in cultures around the world. So have more tangible, documented horrors.

Some of what has gone into this book is based on very real events. Those horrors exist.

The Four Bloodlines

The Four Bloodlines are entirely of my own creation, with certain lycanthropic characteristics based on European legends. Out of respect for cultures that aren't mine, I do not include any references to non-European shapeshifters of any kind in the Rising Bloodlines trilogy. It would be a terrible and presumptuous form of cultural theft.

Besides, and seriously, there are some things you don't mess with.

Indian boarding schools and Karina's identity

In the case of Falling Silver, Karina started out as a throwaway character—as a sort of silly blonde girl in the woods who trips and falls to the jaws of a werewolf in a weak homage to the old

1950s horror movie trope. I never did like that track I was on, and in fact I can't even remember that original character's name. Strange things happen in writers' minds, though. I usually refer to this as "writer's psychosis," and it came to me in a half-dream one night in San Diego when a tall, black-haired young woman knocked on my bedroom door, beelined for my blankets and pillows, sat down and more or less told me to listen up.

"My name is Karina," she said. "My mother was Russian and my father Ojibwe." All right, now I had to have lost my mind. "Pay attention," she continued. "You're missing the real story here. The real monsters. Remember middle school in Canada?"

Oh, my. I knew exactly what Karina was talking about. I remembered clearly the classmates who had been taken from their Indigenous families and placed with Anglo ones, and sent to the same day school I attended. They kept to themselves, and I asked one of the other white girls at my school why they seemed so sad and angry. When she explained it to me, I flat-out didn't believe it. She gave me more details, and it dawned on me that this was not the usual tall tale related to the new kid in school to see how gullible they were. This was quite, quite real.

I still had vestiges of my Scottish accent at the age of eleven, and that meant I was strange enough to my schoolmates that I had already experienced my own (minor, compared with this discussion) run-ins with bullying teachers and school kids.

Believe it or not, that was once acceptable. I was just different enough to wonder if the authorities would come for me and my brothers, to split us up and make us live with families we didn't know so that we would learn to be more Canadian.

By the time I got home I was in tears, and I begged my mother not to let them take us away. She had no idea what I was talking about, but clearly I believed it, so she called the school. We had only one or two further discussions about the topic, but I will never forget the grim set of her mouth when she realized it was true. And I will never, ever be able to fathom the despair and anger of the families who not only feared this, but lived it, with no possibility of going to a safe, familiar home and nobody to help them.

I include references to these institutions in Falling Silver through the fictitious Catlinite School, which I based loosely on the Pipestone School (also known as the Pipestone Indian Training School) in Minnesota and the infamous Carlisle School in Pennsylvania.

There is a great deal of historical content available on this subject, with photos that will tear up your soul when you look into the eyes of the children whose hair has been cut, their language forbidden, and their entire support system removed.

These details don't appear in Falling Silver, because while it's vital for us all to know about these stories, they are not mine to relate. It's not possible to tell them the way I've heard them personally from the people who have survived it. To go into that here would be superficial and therefore disrespectful, so I am including some resources below. I urge readers to explore this subject properly, through historical resources that will more accurately reflect the truth than I possibly could on these pages.

The practice of removing children from their families and placing them in boarding schools for "assimilation" continued in the United States until 1969, and in Canada until 1996.

Resources to get you started:

The Carlisle Indian School (Pennsylvania)

One of the most infamous of all, Carlisle's "re-education" institution was founded upon Captain Richard Henry Pratt's recommendation to "Kill the Indian in him and save the man." This tells you something about the concept but does not justify either its existence or its purpose. For more information about the school, please visit the link below for the Digital Resource Center.

Link: https://carlisleindian.dickinson.edu/teach/kill-indian-him-and-save-man-r-h-pratt-education-native-americans

The Pipestone Indian Training School (Minnesota)

There is an extensive library of records and photographs available about this institution. I refer to the "Catlinite School," which is completely fictitious, but I did use the term "Catlinite" because it is the scientific name for pipestone.

Links:

Pipestone County Museum:
https://pipestonecountymuseum.com/pipestone-indian-
training-school/

Minnesota Digital Library:
https://collection.mndigital.org/catalog?f[subject_ssim][]=Pip
estone%20Indian%20Training%20School

From *Minnpost.com*, July 2024:
https://www.minnpost.com/greater-
minnesota/2024/07/records-shed-light-on-pipestone-indian-
boarding-school/

If you don't actually know someone with first-hand experience, the best places to start with Indigenous cultural
questions are tribal outreach offices. For different projects I've
worked on, I've called various tribal public information
personnel with what I've felt were dumb or embarrassing
questions. Every time, I have been told that asking the people
who can actually tell me the truth is both welcome and
appreciated. Nobody is going to try and make you feel silly,
guilty or responsible. These are first steps anyone can take to
ensuring that it doesn't happen again.

Japanese Internment Camps, WWII

Almost immediately after the attack on Pearl Harbor on
December 7th of 1941, the U.S. removed Japanese and Japa-

nese-American families from their homes and lands in the United States. There was little or no warning, and people were relocated to distant and uncomfortable camps for the duration of the war. Many stayed on afterward in the places they were taken, while others returned home to find that the government had appropriated their farmlands and other financially interesting property.

Santa Fe, New Mexico, with all the beauty it radiates in the present day, hosted a remarkably little-known internment camp which was located near what is now Frank S. Ortiz Park. I did take historical liberties with the Santa Fe camp, as there was only one and it was restricted to men only. In a different camp, Sayuri might have found herself in a similar situation, in that she might have been separated from her brother and other male family members.

Resources:

Encyclopedia Britannica (overview)
https://www.britannica.com/event/Japanese-American-internment

New Mexico History Museum
https://nmhistorymuseum.org/exhibition/details/5004/stories-memories-and-legacies

Santa Fe New Mexican newspaper archives; includes interviews with internment camp survivors. Digital access may require a subscription.

https://santafenewmexican.newspaperarchive.com/tags/internment-camp/

The Migrant Camp

When I worked for the online department of a major newspaper in California, along the U.S.-Mexico border, part of my job involved handling our division's reader emails. One frantic message arrived from a local man who owned property that he said was clearly being used to house human-trafficking camps. He described the presence of young women and girls there, along with the rough shelters and the restraints used to imprison them. For many reasons, law enforcement agencies either could not or would not help him, he told me by phone. This man was nearly in tears as he explained his evidence of what was happening there and the helplessness he felt. When I brought this to one of the editors for a possible investigative story, he could not assist, either. All I can do is bring you Lucia, a fictitious representative of this very real and ongoing situation.

Resources:

How to report human trafficking:
https://www.dhs.gov/blue-campaign/report-human-trafficking

Call:

Homeland Security Investigations tip line at 1-866-347-2423.

National Human Trafficking Hotline at 1-888-373-7888.

Get to know your neighbors

I'm a big fan of talking to people. I strongly encourage you to contact international and local cultural societies in your area to let them know of your interest in broadening your knowledge. You might ask about festivals, exhibits, musical performances, and more that might be held in your neighborhood. Ask about people's favorite writers, musicians, and artists, and then look into those. It doesn't have to be a different culture, either. Just get to know your neighbors.

"We're a' Jock Tamson's bairns."

So goes the Scottish saying that my father taught me. Our family moved often because of Dad's work. Both he and my mother encouraged us to learn about our new surroundings, including the history and cultures of the people whose worlds we were entering, and of others where the family had lived before we were born. These words from my original homeland underscore the joys of discovering that we are all, in truth, the children of our Creator, Maker, the Almighty, Science—and of how much we have in common. It's exhilarating!

Let's leave the monsters on the page, and try not to look for reasons to tear each other up.

Made in USA - Kendallville, IN
97082_9781983047138
10.23.2024 2138